NO PLACE TO LIVE

The mutilated body had been identified as ex-mobster Frank Hamilton. Frankie had been planning to run off with $400,000 in racket money — but when the body was found, the money wasn't. Many of Frankie's former associates showed up to search his old apartment. Reporter Jerry Benedict got in first, but he wasn't alone: there was a still-warm corpse on the bed, a man with a sharp spike through his heart — Frank Hamilton!

*Books by Edward S. Aarons
in the Linford Mystery Library:*

ASSIGNMENT PALERMO
THEY ALL RAN AWAY
ASSIGNMENT TO DISASTER
SAY IT WITH MURDER

EDWARD S. AARONS

NO PLACE TO LIVE

Complete and Unabridged

LINFORD
Leicester

First published in the
United States of America

First Linford Edition
published October 1994

British Library CIP Data

Aarons, Edward S.
No place to live.—Large print ed.—
Linford mystery library
I. Title II. Series
813.54 [F]

ISBN 0–7089–7628–X

Published by
F. A. Thorpe (Publishing) Ltd.
Anstey, Leicestershire

Set by Words & Graphics Ltd.
Anstey, Leicestershire
Printed and bound in Great Britain by
T. J. Press (Padstow) Ltd., Padstow, Cornwall

This book is printed on acid-free paper

For
BILL and ESTELLE

1

BAKERMAN leaned both elbows on the oak desk and spoke casually into the telephone. "Dulcey's office. Yeah, this is Harvey." Bakerman was a detective, second grade, and he looked like a tired haberdasher's clerk. His gray hair was neatly parted in the middle, and he wore a faded cardigan sweater under his loose serge suit. A buttery electric light in the ceiling made craggy shadows around his mouth as he spoke into the phone. "Who'd you say? Oh, Jerry! Sure, come on up."

He cradled the telephone without lifting his elbows, then swiveled to sit on the edge of the desk. His partner, Pease, was staring through the window at the rainy street. An electric clock on the yellow wall read ten-thirty, but it hadn't been going

1

for a month. It was past four in the afternoon, and the street beyond the dusty window was prematurely dark in the rain.

Pease said: "Look at it come down. Jeez, how I hate it." He sneezed abruptly and sat on the gurgling radiator. "I ought to go to Florida. It's too damned cold up here."

There was an unhealthy glitter in his dark, smudged eyes. Most of the time he hated Bakerman and hated his job, but occasionally he found compensation that would have interested a psychoanalyst. He adjusted himself on the sputtering radiator and hugged his thin chest.

"Who was that on the phone?"

"Jerry Benedict. That cartoonist fellow. He's coming up."

"To see Cy?"

"He's got a dame with him," Bakerman said. He looked at the useless electric clock on the wall, and consulted his own pocket watch. "I guess he wants to impress her."

2

Pease sneezed again. "Them reporters," he sighed.

"Jerry's all right. He's no reporter. He's just filling in on Tullen's beat."

"Jerry is a screwball," Pease said. "Them cartoons he draws are plenty screwy."

The rain made a rattling sound against the dirty window. The office was big and barren, and smelled strongly of stale cigar smoke and disinfectant. The windows overlooked the green globes lighting the precinct station entrance, two floors down. On the frosted glass door was painted Lieutenant Cy Dulcey's name, and under that, the words *Homicide Division*.

One side of the room was walled with glass partitions shielding Lieutenant Dulcey's inner office. It was more or less soundproofed, and the two people in there now went through a pantomime conversation inaudible to the two detectives. Dulcey sat at his desk, short, squat, and infinitely patient. The girl had her back to the glass partitions, and the two detectives could see only the cloth collar of her coat and the dark hair that tumbled down over her shoulders. Her legs were crossed and she sat quite still, answering Dulcey's interminable queries. Pease was content with what he glimpsed of the girl's legs.

"Half an hour already," he sighed. "He ain't getting anywhere with that female."

Bakerman said: "Dulcey's no dope. Routine breaks them all down, sooner or later." He made himself comfortable in a swivel chair and stared morosely at the yellow ceiling. "Wish I was home now — a rotten day like this."

"You and your home." Pease was a bachelor; he had lived at the same hotel for the past ten years, and hated it. "All you do is take orders from your old lady."

"Well, maybe I like it," Bakerman said, unperturbed. He took his feet down from the open drawer as the outer door opened and Jerry Benedict came in, guiding a girl. "Hi, Jeremiah."

Jerry Benedict said: "Hello, Harvey." He glanced at Pease. "Still got your cold?"

"I always got a cold," Pease complained. "It's hanging around this dump that gives it to me." He looked at the girl and the glitter brightened in his dark, smudged eyes. "You newspaper guys get all the breaks."

"This is Patti Duggan," Jerry said. He held the girl's arm gently and performed brief introductions. "She's never been in a police station before."

"I'll bet," said Pease.

Jerry Benedict ignored him and glanced through the glass partition into the inner office. Lieutenant Dulcey was still talking to the girl. "Who's that?"

"The boss. He says he's working."

"But the girl?"

Bakerman said lazily: "You should worry, Jerry."

Jerry Benedict shrugged. He was a tall man with red hair under a battered, rain-sodden hat. The lapels of

5

his raincoat were open to reveal a dark knitted tie and a soft white shirt with the collar button missing. His face was thin, his eyes clear. He looked about twenty-five, and was actually thirty.

"Make yourself comfortable, Patti," he said to the girl. He kept looking through the glass windows of Dulcey's office, trying to see the other girl's face. Detective Pease got off the radiator and sat down on a battered leather couch against the wall. The girl seated herself timidly beside him.

Pease said: "So you never been inside a police station before, that right?"

The girl nodded and cast an anguished glance at Jerry Benedict. She had lemon-colored hair and wore a dark felt hat that shaded her eyes. Her face looked wan. Her mouth was richly lipsticked, and trembling. "Jerry thought it would be interesting."

"Jerry ought to stick to his drawing board," Pease said. "He ought to stick to them screwball cartoons he makes for the *Globe*, instead of playing legman for

Tullen. One of these days he's going to run into an egg-beater and get slapped down."

Bakerman said: "Ah, what do you know about it, Peasey?"

"All I know," Pease said, "is the administration blows a gasket every time one of Jerry's pictures gets printed in the *Globe*."

"I didn't know you looked at the editorial page," Jerry said mildly.

Bakerman grinned. "Jerry's all right, Peasey. He just likes to tilt his pen at windmills."

Pease looked puzzled. He sneezed violently, and Patti Duggan edged a little away from him on the couch.

"Anyway," Pease said, "a cartoonist got no business messing into murder cases. Remember the Phillip Mattson killin'? You and me did all the work, and Jerry just tagged along, getting in everybody's hair; but it was Dulcey who grabbed all the credit."

Bakerman said drily: "You mean it was Jerry solved the case and we just mushed around."

Pease blew his nose into a soiled handkerchief.

"Jerry'd cut his mother's throat for a new angle," he said. "He wasn't ethical."

The girl said nothing. Her troubled eyes watched Jerry as he drifted across the office to a bank of file cabinets and opened the top drawer.

"Like to look at some case files, Patti?"

Bakerman drawled: "Just keep your hands the hell out of there, Jerry. That's official records."

"They're open to the press, aren't they?" Jerry asked. He took a manila folder from the second file and dropped it in the girl's lap. Pease looked uncertain, his protest cut off by Bakerman's shrug. Jerry stared at Dulcey's figure beyond the glass partition.

"Who is the girl with the black hair?" he asked again. "She looks familiar."

Pease laughed. "Dulcey keeps her

around long enough. Maybe he just likes to look at her."

Jerry said: "Well, I've seen her somewhere before. She gives me butterflies."

"Sure," said Pease. "You seen her at the morgue. She was one of Frankie Hamilton's chippies."

Jerry whistled in astonishment. "That gorgeous beast?"

"Anyway, she knew him," Bakerman corrected. "Name is Stephanie Farley, and we caught her snooping around Frankie the Foot's apartment the day after we found his body. She said she was just a good friend, that's all."

Pease licked his lips. "She should be a good friend to me, is what I'd like."

Jerry said: "Isn't she the one who identified what was left of the senator when you fished him out of the river?"

Bakerman nodded. "Only you better not call Frankie the Foot a senator, Jerry. Some of the real ones might object."

9

There came a sudden gasp from Patti Duggan. She stood up, wavered, and said: "Mr. Benedict, I — " The case file slid from her fingers and splashed to her feet in a cascade of typewritten reports and glossy photographs. Her face was ghastly in the wan electric light. She moaned, and crumpled all in a heap to the floor.

Bakerman said: "What the hell?" and just stared.

Jerry crossed the room with a swift stride, picked up the girl, and placed her gingerly on the worn leather couch. Her body felt thin and boneless in his arms. He began slapping gently at her wrists and cheeks.

"She's fainted," he muttered.

Pease gathered up the spill of papers. He straightened suddenly, and sneezed with abrupt violence.

"No wonder," he said harshly. "You showed her the morgue pix of Frankie Hamilton — what was left of him, I mean." Pease looked at the girl's disarranged dress.

"She ain't such a bad little chippie, at that."

Bakerman snarled: "Why don't you get married? Then you could keep your mind on your work."

"I don't notice you lookin' the other way," Pease smirked.

Jerry arranged the girl's skirt. There came the slam of a door and the heavy, angry footsteps of Lieutenant Dulcey.

"What are you doing here, Benedict?"

"I'm taking Tullen's job. He's on vacation."

"You're a cartoonist, not a legman." The squat lieutenant looked sharply at the girl on the couch. "What's all this?"

The dark-haired girl, Stephanie Farley, had vanished from his office beyond the glass panels. Evidently Dulcey had rushed her out by a direct door to the corridor. Jerry turned apologetically to the homicide lieutenant.

"I'm sorry, Cy. I was just showing the lady some pix, and she fainted."

"Pictures of Frankie the Foot,"

11

Bakerman said coolly.

"You let him have them?" Dulcey snapped.

"You said we shouldn't stop any newsmen if they looked. You said we should only discourage 'em." Bakerman added: "The dame is Patti Duggan, lieutenant."

"Never heard of her," Dulcey said. He was short and stocky, and his blue eyes were filigree with little veins. He was forty-two, and had gone up in the Force with astounding rapidity, due to a combination of ruthless persistence, and the keen, agile mind of a hunter who made the city his natural habitat. He bobbed a little on his saddle-soaped shoes, confronting the girl as she sat up.

"I'm so sorry," she murmured. "It was stupid to faint."

"What did Jerry put you up to?" Dulcey demanded.

"He didn't put me up to anything," the girl whispered. She began to sob once more, soundlessly.

Jerry said softly: "Patti. Patti, listen to me. Were those pictures of Frank Hamilton?"

"She shook her head quickly. "No."

"Who was it?"

"It was Johnny Lisbon."

Dulcey's face was dark with anger. "What are you talking about? Those are pictures of Frankie the Foot, just as we pulled him out of the river. Where does Johnny Lisbon fit?"

Jerry said: "Patti was Lisbon's girl. And Johnny Lisbon used to be one of Hamilton's boys, when Frank ran his little drug racket — before he turned 'respectable' and became known as 'The Investor' for other racket bosses, by putting their money into real estate and stocks and bonds — little cover-ups like legitimate investments to show on their tax returns."

"So what? What are you getting at?"

The girl dabbed at her tears.

"Johnny was my fellow," she said. "That is, he was, up to the time

Hamilton made a pass at me. Johnny had a terrible temper, and he had a fight with Hamilton and quit working for him. That was three weeks ago, and I never saw Johnny again."

"Very touching," Dulcey said.

Jerry said: "Look, you had this Stephanie Farley identify the body, and you had Frank's girl, that Wanda Dykes, look at him, too. They both identified it as Frank Hamilton. But he was missing an arm and both legs, and his face didn't look like much more than a squash pie. I just have a hunch, that's all. You heard what Patti Duggan says. That isn't Hamilton's body at all. It was Johnny Lisbon you fished out of the North River."

Dulcey's stare brooded dangerously on Jerry's lean face.

"I ought to throw you into the can for this," he said.

"For what?"

"For taking those files. They're official property."

14

Jerry grinned. "Go ahead and try. You have no charges. I didn't take those files without permission."

"I can hold the girl as a material witness."

Patti Duggan said: "But that *is* Johnny Lisbon!"

"How do you know that?"

"Well I knew Johnny," she said hesitantly. A deep blush suddenly colored her cheeks. "I knew him very well."

"Enough to recognize him from those pictures?"

"He had a mole on his right shoulder," said the girl. "There's a mole on the shoulder in those photographs, too."

Dulcey grabbed at the file and flipped through the glossy prints, scowling with his thick gray brows. His tie had come loose from the initialed silver clip and dangled between the lapels of his pinstripe suit.

"That isn't a mole. It's just a smudge on the print. A body that's been in the water as long as this one can get all kinds of marks on it. The mole doesn't mean a thing."

Jerry said: "Well, where is Johnny Lisbon, then?"

"What do I care?" Dulcey snapped. His pale blue eyes rested angrily on Jerry. "I'm not interested in listening to your bright ideas or seeing you around my office. If you had any notions on the case, you could have come to me with them in the first place."

"That's just it," Jerry said. "How far would I get? Especially after that last series of cartoons I drew about the uptown muggings. You wouldn't let me past your door. If you did, the commissioner would lift your scalp; he doesn't think I flattered him. I'm strictly *persona non grata* around here, and you know it."

Dulcey still looked dangerous. "Tullen was willing to play ball; but I can't count on you. You're too unpredictable."

"I draw and write what I see," Jerry

said stubbornly. "And I see where you didn't identify that body properly."

Dulcey said: "As a matter of fact, we've known that body isn't Frank Hamilton's for several days. Our lab men told us that. I just wanted to find out who wants us to think Frank Hamilton is dead, and why. I hope that satisfies you. And now you can get out."

"Both of us? No jail?"

"Are you asking for it?" Dulcey rapped.

"Not at all," Jerry said quickly.

Bakerman and Pease were at the door as he guided the girl out. The gaunt detective gave Jerry a concealed wink.

"See you in the funny papers, son."

Downstairs, Jerry paused inside the swinging street doors and looked for a cab on the rainy avenue.

Patti Duggan said: "Those cops didn't like you, Jerry."

Jerry patted her hand. He looked back into the precinct station, saw no one around, and took a wallet from his pocket, took out several folded bills. "You were swell, Patti; you did a fine job. Your faint even had me fooled. At least, we gave them something to think about."

The girl pushed back the money.

"I don't want it, Jerry. You made a deal with me to stick a needle into the cops. That's always a pleasure, so I agreed."

"That's right," Jerry said.

"No, that's wrong." Patti's dark felt hat shaded her eyes. Her red mouth trembled. "I'm scared to death, which shows I have more sense than you."

"Scared?"

"Somebody is trying to convince the cops that Frank Hamilton is dead. So I'm staying out of it. I'm fond of living."

"I don't get it," Jerry said. "I told you to help me needle Dulcey, sure. I told you to act as if that body was really Johnny Lisbon's, and not Frank Hamilton."

"But something went wrong," said the girl.

"What went wrong?"

"I wasn't acting," she said. "It was really Johnny."

2

GIUSEPPE, head waiter at the Rock Garden, grinned and said: "For my wife. I tell her alla time about you."

He offered a napkin and stubby black crayon to Jerry. Jerry put aside his halibut steak and with a few deft strokes, a subtle distortion of nose, chin and facial planes, added to a brief suggestion of a bellying apron, and Giuseppe was reproduced on the napkin.

"That's the way you look to me, Josie," Jerry said.

Giuseppe cocked his head dubiously. "That a fact? My wife think you a great artist, Mist' Benedict." He scowled and grew confidential. "You get fired, or something?"

"The hell," Jerry said. "I'm only pinch-hitting on the police beat."

He finished his ale, left a bill for his check, and went out into the rain. It was after five when he reached the Globe building. The city room was empty except for Sparling at the rewrite desk. Sparling was thin and sandy-haired, with a savage mouth and disillusioned eyes. In ten years he had managed to become assistant to the night editor. His white collar gleamed primly in the glow of the tin-shaded lamps.

"Boss wants to see you," he advised. "Squawking his pants off." Sparling's pale eyes watched the rain drip from Jerry's hat. "Seems you should have stuck to your funny drawings. You're in a jam with the cops already."

"Oh, that," Jerry said. "Where is Luscious?"

"Up in the Garden of Eden," Sparling said. He meant the rest lounge which an indulgent publisher had instituted for the feminine help, but which was used indiscriminately by all of the *Globe's* personnel.

McConaughy was alone when Jerry walked in. He lay mountainously on a deep leather couch, his head resting on thick, folded arms, his eyes fixed dreamily on the paneled ceiling. The walls were decorated with pastel sporting prints of spindle-legged dogs and horses, blowups of the *Globe's* photographic beats of the past year, and pencil caricatures of all the staff, done by Jerry. A blonde girl in an angora sweater came out of the door marked *Ladies* and said, "Hi, Jerry. The Beast has been waiting for you." McConaughy merely flicked a glance at her as she swayed out. Jerry said, "Well, here I am, Mr. McConaughy. It was a tough fight. They had me cornered, and one of them had a scimitar four feet long. But I ate my Krunchies and fought clear to report to you." He held up one hand in a mock salute. "The nation is saved."

McConaughy said: "You drunk?" He was an enormously fat man, with a great round moon of a face and a shock of curly brown hair. His shirt sleeves were anchored above his dimpled elbows by a pair of lady's pink garters, adorned with ivory roses. He said, "Oh, God," apropos of nothing at all, and wheezed erect. "I'll have to reduce. I hate to, but I'm over two-eighty now."

Jerry shook his head. "You won't even cast a shadow, if your sylph-like figure gets more sylph-like."

"Shut up," said McConaughy. He reached with dimpled hands for a cigar and carefully peeled the cellophane wrapper. His eyes were cocked critically on the tall reporter. "You laid an egg."

Jerry said: "The hell I did."

"You're an artist, my boy. Not a detective," said McConaughy. He liked the paternal sound of his voice. "Yes, son, talent such as yours shouldn't be wasted on leg work. You will go back to your drawing board, as of now."

Jerry said seriously: "I don't get it."

"Let us say that you are withdrawn from circulation until the Hamilton case simmers down. Lieutenant Dulcey just telephoned to bar you from all official investigations, henceforth and forever and one day."

Jerry said bitterly: "Listen, Dulcey's just sore because I got the jump on him. I showed Patti Duggan the files on Hamilton and she backed me to the hilt. Frank Hamilton wasn't hit. He's still alive, probably sitting on his fanny somewhere and laughing his head off, thinking of the cops closing the books on him. That rat is scot-free, and the body which Dulcey pretended was so precious is really Frank's former rod man, one John Lisbon. Patti identified it positively, and she ought to know. What's more, Dulcey knew it and was trying to keep it from the press, for reasons of his own."

McConaughy considered his enormous belly and shook his head.

"No dice, Jerry. Normally, I wouldn't let Dulcey dictate which men I should send to cover a story. But this broth looks poisonous, and you're too valuable to the *Globe* to let me risk you on it."

"It's my story," Jerry said stubbornly. "All I need is to convince the Duggan girl that she'll be protected if she testifies. You can't take me off it now, Lucius."

"I can't, but I'm doing it. You go back to your drawing board and the editorial page tomorrow. I hate to admit it, but the boss thinks you're one of the most valuable men on the paper. We've got an honest, aggressive publisher, Jerry, and he liked your campaign on the investment of criminal profits from the Cosa Nostra, Mafia, and whatever, in housing projects, hotels, banks and other legitimate real estate. Just one of your silly little cartoons draws more blood than a whole page full of editorials. It's not Dulcey who's taking you off the case. It's the boss himself. You go back to cartoons tomorrow."

"Well, wrap me in silk and call me a cocoon," Jerry said bitterly.

"Tomorrow? What about tonight? Why the delay?"

"Get drunk and forget it," McConaughy advised.

Jerry hesitated, then slammed the door angrily on his way out. McConaughy lay back on the couch and puffed meditatively at his cigar. Alone, his big stomach rippled gently as he laughed to himself.

* * *

Tillie Adams, one of the girls from the classified ad department, was leaning on Jerry's drawing board when he returned to the city room. She was studying an early edition of the *Globe*, spread out under her hands. Jerry took a handkerchief and flicked it to sting her most prominent feature. She didn't move.

"No sense, no feeling," he said.

"You're right about the last part." Tillie tossed her head. "It's lucky for you I keep my eyes open, Mr. Benedict.

26

I've got something for you."

"Wrap it up and put it in the icebox, lamb," Jerry said.

"But this is serious." She folded the newspaper, and he saw that she had been studying the real estate classified ads. "Aren't you working on the Hamilton case?"

Jerry thought about it. "Until tomorrow, I guess."

"Didn't Hamilton live downtown somewhere? On Waverly Walk, wasn't it?"

"Number 16," Jerry said. "What's teasing you?"

"It's for rent," she said triumphantly.

"I suppose that ends the rent control housing shortage," he said glumly.

"Well, don't you understand?" She pretended great exasperation. "Honestly, I don't see where you get your reputation for being so smart. Hamilton's apartment is for rent. See?"

"Jerry said: "Well, hell, why didn't you say so?" He took the newspaper from her and stared at the classified ad she indicated. It looked quite ordinary:

> *WAVERLEY WALK, No. 16,*
> *frnshd, 3 rms, bth, 1st flr.*
> *$150, Apply Gantredi, supt.*

Tillie said complacently: "I just happened to notice it. And after that girl asked about it, I marked it for you."

Jerry said abruptly:

"What girl? Who asked about this ad?"

"She didn't give any name, and she didn't ask exactly about this one. She didn't know it had been filed already. But she wanted to know if No. 16 Waverly Walk was advertised for rent, and she wanted a peek at the column in advance. I didn't let her, because Johnson was hanging around."

"When was all this?"

"About twenty minutes ago. I think she's downstairs now, waiting for this edition to hit the streets."

Jerry swiveled around his desk and went to the window. Just outside the entrance to the Globe Building was O'Ryan's news stand. Pedestrians bobbed along under twin streams of umbrellas as he stared down into the gloomy evening. A girl in a plastic rain cape waited impatiently near the news stand. He couldn't see her face or anything about her except that her hair was very dark and thick and shining on her shoulders. She looked very much like the girl he had seen in Lieutenant Dulcey's office.

He glanced desperately at his watch. The edition she was waiting for was due to hit the street at five, exactly. He had a three minutes' start. Tillie Adams regarded him with startled eyes as he humped his shoulders into his wet trenchcoat.

"Where do you think you're going?" she asked.

"To rent an apartment," Jerry said.

3

JERRY BENEDICT leaned over the back of the cab-driver's seat and said: "An extra sawbuck if you make it."

He sat back, restless and impatient, as the cab slithered through the homebound traffic on the wet streets, shaking itself like a tired old dog in the rain. A red taxi, a block behind them, clung grimly to their heels.

"What's that address again?" asked the cab-driver.

"Number 16, Waverly Walk. Step on it."

"I'm stepping, mister. It's the hack what's stubborn."

The windshield wiper clacked furiously as they paused for a traffic light. The rain came down in lazy, whispering curtains that clouded the windows with fine moisture. Jerry sat on the very edge of the back seat and anxiously twisted his head to observe the cab behind them. Stephanie Farley had taken off from O'Ryan's news stand outside the Globe Building only a split second after the Five-Star edition hit the sidewalk. She was sticking as close as a mustard plaster, and making no effort to conceal it.

Jerry's taxi slid around the corner of Harvey Street into the narrow entrance to Waverly Walk. The cab-driver slammed on the brakes, the wheels locked, and they glided to the curb like a surf-rider coming ashore.

"Here you are, mister. Number 16, like you said."

Waverly Walk was a placid lagoon hidden away from the eddy of downtown business streets. At its dead end was an archaic Colonial gas-lamp, its glass windows flickering feebly in the dusk. The faded brick houses that bordered the cobblestone walk looked like a scene from one of Hogarth's etchings. The rain was colder, Jerry reflected, than a witch's kiss.

He checked the faded gilt numbers in the Georgian doorway, turned up the collar of his coat, and went down three steps to the entrance. The pursuing cab squawked to a halt behind him. He allowed himself a victorious grin at the disconsolate girl who stood on the sidewalk, sensing her anger as she stared at him in the dusk, then pushed open the lobby door and walked in. No one else was there. The girl couldn't challenge his priority rights.

The lobby was long and narrow and silent, with peach walls and a red mohair bench and a tinted mirror beside the ivory-painted stairway. Jerry hesitated between the only two doors visible. One was obviously an apartment entrance, although there was no card in the brass bracket under the bell. The other door was in an alcove under the stairway. A faded, typewritten card read, *G. Gantredi, Supt.* Both doors were firmly closed.

He sought the superintendent's bell, found none, and rapped. The street door slammed behind him, followed by a gust of cold moist air. Then the girl's footsteps made a quick tattoo as she crossed the lobby floor. Jerry turned to face her.

"After me," he smiled.

"Oh, please," she said.

"Nothing doing. I got here first."

The girl brushed rain from her coat. "My mother always told me the age of chivalry was dead."

"It died with me," Jerry nodded.

She was wearing a dull green topcoat under her plastic raincape and hood. She pushed back the hood and shook her dark hair straight. Her eyes were a calm, deep blue; her nose was a trifle arrogant, tiny and tilted. Miss Farley was in her early twenties, Jerry guessed, taller than average, with a poise and assurance that was almost professional. He took off his hat.

Her voice was throaty.

"Perhaps you won't like this apartment. I really do need a place to live — and you know how things are. What I don't understand is how you beat me here. I paid the man at the news stand a dollar for the first copy of the evening edition. It took me just ten seconds to read all the classified ads, and I had a taxi waiting. How did you do it?"

"I bribed the circulation boys, *inside*, the building," Jerry said. "That gave me a start."

The girl looked depressed. She glanced beyond him, curiously, at the closed door.

"Isn't anyone here to rent the place?"

"Apparently not," he said.

"Are you going to wait?"

"All night, if necessary. Why not try some other ad?"

"You know very well there aren't any other vacancies," Stephanie Farley retorted. "Certainly none in this low rent control area. I don't suppose it would do any good to point out that

34

this is a first-floor apartment, and that my mother is an invalid and that we must — "

"No good at all," Jerry said.

She looked at him calmly. "You're so generous."

She tried the superintendent's door herself, but again there was no answer. They waited in hostile silence. Presently the street door opened and a little man in an oversize raincoat came tottering in. He took off his glasses, fogged with rain, and peered around the lobby with an elfin expression on his round, plump little face.

"I beg your pardon," he said. "Is the vat still flacant?"

Stephanie said: "What kind of language is that?"

The newcomer giggled. His voice was high and flutey, as if he had just finished a fast race.

"My wife sent me to rent this apartment," he said.

"You've been drinking," said Stephanie.

"My word. Can you tell?"

He sat down abruptly on the bench, blinking large, childish eyes. Jerry glanced at the girl, shrugged, and turned as the lobby door opened again. Several people entered at once.

"Comes the stampede," murmured Stephanie.

The little man jumped up and moved democratically.

"C'mon in," he invited happily. He introduced himself with a flourish that made him stagger. "I'm Oliver Finchley, Incorporated. Poin the jarty — I mean, join the party."

Jerry didn't laugh. His stomach quivered and tied itself into a cold knot. One glance at the first newcomer brought a swift, bitter montage of memories. Months in the Cuban Sierra Madre mountains, disillusionment, and ugly, brutal weeks in one of Fidel's concentration camps after the revolution had been sold out to Moscow — all this was not easily forgotten.

The newcomer was a tall South American with dark, gray-streaked hair clinging damply to his flat, aristocratic forehead. An enormous ruby winked on his slender index finger. His amused glance slid past the babbling Mr. Finchley and settled on Jerry for a flickering moment. There was no sign of recognition. Señor Pedro de Ordas, one-time commandant of Castro's prison camps, ex-hatchet man from the Argentine, and now a fugitive himself from Fidel's windy vengeance, would not remember one prisoner from among many helpless thousands.

None of the others were discouraged by Gantredi's absence. A young couple, who identified themselves as Mr. and Mrs. Jason Holovacs, of High Corners, Kansas, promptly huddled on the stairs and clung to each other like babes in the wood, watching everyone with wide, naive interest. The man, with pale watery eyes and a deep scar on his neck, was older by ten years than his wife, whose gamine face was alert and watchful. They blushed and refused a bottle which Finchley pressed on them.

Señor de Ordas rested his slender hands on the head of a walking stick and studied Jerry with large, liquid eyes.

Another apartment-hunter entered the lobby. This one swept in with all the regal assurance of a duchess. She was a tall taffy blonde dressed in a tight satin raincoat belted snugly about her shapely figure, with a spangled turban and a white silk scarf. Her eyes swept the assembled group with imperious disdain. Her earrings tinkled as she turned her head sharply toward Señor de Ordas. He introduced himself in flawless Oxford as coming from the Argentine, explained the delay in locating the rental agent, and pointed out Jerry as being the first one there.

Jerry didn't know if Wanda Dykes recognized him or not. He was thankful he had kept in the background when they met previously at police headquarters. The blonde's perfume was heady, thick with the scent of magnolias; the bells in her ears gave off tiny silvery sounds as she crossed the lobby toward him.

"I'd like to talk to you," she said. Then she noticed Stephanie Farley, and looked startled. "Oh, hello, there."

"Hello, yourself," said Stephanie. She was not enthusiastic. "It's no use, Miss Dykes — this man is taking Frank's apartment. He got here first."

The taffy blonde turned back to Jerry. Her smile was dazzling. "If I could talk to you alone," she said. "Just for a little. Please?"

"I doubt if you can work it," Stephanie said. She went away, seating herself on the stairway. Jerry, following her with his eyes, was surprised to note that the couple from Kansas had apparently vanished into thin air.

Wanda Dykes assumed a businesslike tone.

"I'm sure we can reach some mutual agreement, Mr. — "

"Benedict," said Jerry.

She frowned. "You look familiar."

"It's a common face," Jerry said. "But it's all mine."

Wanda smiled. "Well, of course.

You know, I really must have this apartment."

"But you already have an apartment, Miss Dykes."

She was pleased. "Then you know who I am?"

"Your publicity agent earns his ten percent. You're Wanda Dykes, the toast of the nightclub circuit. Besides, your picture was in all the papers recently, in connection with the disappearance of Frank Hamilton."

The pleased look was abruptly replaced by a pout.

"That was all a nasty, nasty mistake. The police . . . "

"They said you were Frank Hamilton's — er — fiancée."

Caution edged into the blonde's voice now. Her eyes became bleak emeralds intent on Jerry's bland face. She said sharply: "Are you a policeman — "

"I'm just a prospective tenant," Jerry assured her.

"All right, then," Wanda Dykes said. "I'm not here to discuss my affairs with you. I want to buy your right to rent this apartment first. I could go over your head with the rental agent, I'm sure, but I'd rather do it this way."

"Do you know that this apartment used to belong to your unfortunate fiancé?" Jerry looked naive.

"I want it," the blonde said stubbornly. "I'm willing to pay a premium for it."

"How much?" Jerry asked.

Wanda Dykes relaxed a little. "Will one hundred do?"

Jerry frowned. "Cheap apartments are hard to get."

"Two hundred," she said tightly.

"Nothing doing."

She edged closer, until she was standing very close to him. Her magnolia perfume made him a little dizzy. The bells in her ears tinkled melodiously, and she spoke in a husky whisper.

"Not for any price?"

"My aching back," Jerry said.

Furious, the blonde snapped: "To hell with you."

Turning, she crossed the lobby in a trail of scent and tinkling, silvery bells. Jerry's glance caught Stephanie's calm, amused face as she watched him from her perch on the stairs. He took a handkerchief and carefully patted his mouth. Wanda's perfume clung to his coat where she had leaned against him.

The door slammed abruptly as another man joined the group.

4

DANGER walked into the room with the new arrival. He was rather short, with a small gray moustache, carefully waxed; gray eyes, and a cold face that looked as if it received a daily massage. He wore a derby and a chesterfield coat, and he kept his hands in his pockets. Under his silk scarf glistened an immaculate shirt front and a maroon bowtie. There was something frozen and catlike about him; he reminded Jerry of a beast of prey, entering a strange place with alert caution. Wanda Dykes looked suddenly stricken at his appearance. She got up suddenly, started to say something, and then sat down again. The newcomer, eyeing Jerry, ignored her.

"They say you were here first," he announced curtly.

Jerry nodded. "I'm just waiting for

the superintendent. There's really no sense in you people hanging around, because I intend to take this apartment, regardless."

The man's face was utterly expressionless.

"Was Miss Dykes trying to bribe you?"

"I don't think it is any of your business."

"Whatever she offered, I'll double it."

"You couldn't," said Jerry, glancing at Wanda's lush figure. "Not in a million years."

"I am prepared to make any reasonable financial offer."

Jerry said: "Then you knew Frank Hamilton, too?"

His question was completely ignored. The gray man took one hand from his pocket and opened it, palm upward, to reveal a thick roll of bills.

"We can strike a bargain, I'm sure."

"Sorry. No sale."

"Perhaps you don't know who I am,"

44

said the gray man.

"I know you," Jerry countered. "You're George Chalett — one of the few gamblers who turn in an honest income tax. That's why you're not in jail — not yet. I guess everybody knows you, Mr. Chalett — or knows about you."

"Then you must know," Chalett said softly, "that I am accustomed to getting what I want."

"Not this time," said Jerry.

A dim cloud of emotion, as vague and intangible as a chill breeze, trembled on the gambler's calm face. He measured Jerry's tall figure objectively.

"You're a rather foolish young man," the gambler observed.

Turning, Chalett studied the lobby, then sat down beside Wanda Dykes. The blonde immediately began whispering to him, her words swift and imperative. The gambler said something abruptly and she turned her back on him, her earrings tinkling.

The sound of rain came dimly from

the cobblestones outside. It was warm inside the lobby. The clock on the wall read six-ten. The street outside was quite dark. Jerry moved purposefully to the door of the vacant apartment.

"We ought to see what we're waiting around for, anyway," he said, and tried the knob. To his surprise, the door swung easily open. There was nothing but a dark, dim, foyer beyond. The others immediately crowded after him. Someone said, surprised: "It's been open all the time!"

Stephanie was right behind him. "After you, Galahad."

They were about to go in when heavy, hurried steps sounded on the second floor stairs, and a woman's odd, deep tones boomed:

"See here! What do you people think you're doing?"

She was enormous, broad of shoulder, and her tweed suit exactly matched her muddy tan face. She made Jerry think of an Amazon — over forty, with thickly braided black hair and large, liquid eyes set in a forbidding face, snapping with anger.

"How do you do?" Jerry murmured. "We've been waiting to see Mr. Gantredi. I just tried the door, and found it open."

The woman said: "I'm Mrs. Lucy Quarles, from upstairs. If you will explain what all you people are doing here — "

"We're answering an ad for this apartment," Jerry said. "But your superintendent seems to have forgotten all about it."

"Indeed," said Mrs. Quarles. Her dark eyes flashed with distaste at the elfishly drunken Mr. Finchley. "I act as sub-agent for these buildings, whenever Mr. Gantredi is away. But since he chose to handle the advertisement without my knowledge, you will just have to wait for him to show up."

Stephanie Farley said: "Well, there's no harm in our looking at the place, is there?"

Jerry didn't wait for an answer from

the Amazon. He pushed inside and snapped on the foyer light. The others trooped after him as he went down two steps into a sunken living room. There was a wide casement window opening on Waverly Walk, and rain pattered on the small leaded panes. Over the white stone fireplace was a huge circular mirror in a gold and silver frame, like a sunburst ornament. A spinet piano stood in one corner of the room. There were relics of a former hot-air heating system in the open grilles sunk into the walls. One of the blue armchairs lay on its back, the bottom ripped out and the stuffing scattered over the rug. The pictures had been taken down from the walls and now rested on the floor. They had no backs. Scores of books were strewn haphazardly against the walnut paneling.

"Looks like a cyclone hit it," Stephanie murmured.

"It was the police," Mrs. Quarles boomed. Her face was a stony mask ravaged by time and eroded by distant storms. "There was a little difficulty here over the last tenant."

Jerry was idly prodding the debris on the floor with his toe. Something glittered on the tiles outside the hearth, and he stooped, picked it up, and examined it. It was a triangular piece of dark celluloid. He put it in his pocket, stepped back a little as Oliver Finchley staggered past, and took Stephanie's arm. A quick pressure of his fingers guided her out of the room. The others remained where they were, grouped uncertainly about the living room. There was a short hallway, a bedroom in an incredible state of upheaval, and a kitchen with dirty dishes stacked in the sink. Jerry paused at the back door, opened it, and looked out at a dark, narrow alley, then turned back to the girl.

"Look here," he said urgently. "For your own good, you'd better get away from this place."

The girl's face was dim in the light

that filtered back from the front of the apartment. Her hands moved restlessly.

"Why should I leave?" she asked quietly.

"I know who you are," Jerry said. "That's why."

"Indeed?"

Jerry rubbed his forehead where the rain had splashed him. "You sound just like Mrs. Quarles. What you don't seem to grasp is that some of these people were intimately connected with Frank Hamilton, before he disappeared. And they are all peculiarly anxious to rent Frank Hamilton's apartment. Doesn't that suggest anything to you?"

Stephanie looked at the dirty dishes in the sink.

"No, it doesn't suggest a thing. Should it?"

"They might recognize you," Jerry said. "It would be dangerous. You see, I know that you were in Lt. Dulcey's office not two hours ago. And you identified a body recently as being Frank Hamilton's."

She wasn't surprised. Her laughter was soft and amused.

"Did I?" she asked. "You're pretty good, you know. You think you can frighten me off and leave you free to rent this place, all by yourself. It's a wonderful apartment, though, and I've been looking too long to be scared off now. Besides, I never heard of Frank Hamilton before tonight."

It seemed incredible that she could lie as beautifully as she looked. Jerry flipped his hand downward in a gesture of dismissal.

"It's your funeral," he said.

She looked at him seriously and challenged: "Just where do you fit into all this? How do you know about the former tenant? You don't look like a detective, but you most certainly ask a lot of questions."

"I'm not a detective," he said. His tall figure was a motionless shadow in the kitchen, in an attitude of listening. After a moment, he added: "You'd better wait here a moment," and returned to

51

the hall. From the living room came the murmur of the others' voices. Oliver Finchley, Inc., was obviously passing the bottle. He hesitated, then opened the door into a room furnished as a study. A small kidney desk stood in the alcove of a bay window; there was a red leather couch and a white telephone with a pink plastic dial. The furniture here was just as disarranged as in the other rooms. Jerry dropped his wet hat on the couch, picked up the white phone and dialed a number with quick fingers.

He was halfway through when he heard a faint click in the receiver. He stopped dialing and listened, said, "Hello?"

There came another faint click, then just the dial tone hummed in his ear. Abruptly he replaced the instrument without completing his call.

There were two closet doors in the room. Inside the first, he was greeted by the dull glitter of a small, knee-high safe. The closet was crammed with abandoned personal belongings: forty-dollar shoes, an English topcoat, five rather flashy but expensive suits with Fifth Avenue labels, a row of hats on the shelf above, and a battered concertina crammed into a corner. Evidently the closet had been added to the room after the heating system had been changed, for there was another hot-air grille set in the back wall. Jerry scowled and dropped to his knees before the safe. It was securely locked. There were file marks corrugating the gleaming dial, as if someone had tried, quite clumsily, to get the safe open, and failed.

From behind him came Stephanie Farley's tart voice:

"Any luck, Galahad?"

Jerry got to his feet, dusting his knees. The girl smiled and closed the corridor door. The sound of Señor Pedro de Ordas' voice was abruptly cut off, and so was most of the light. Her voice came softly out of the darkness.

"What are you looking for?"

"Once," Jerry sighed, "I lived in a

house that had a locked closet under the cellar stairs, and after a while I got curious enough to have it opened for me, just to see what was inside."

"And what did you find?"

"Brandy," said Jerry. "Bottles and bottles of fine old Napoleon brandy. I've been hopeful ever since. Opening closets has become a monomania with me."

"Well, what are we waiting for?" she asked.

But the second closet was stubbornly locked. Jerry paused, fumbled about the dark room, and found a three-way reflector lamp, and turned it on low. There were venetian blinds over the bay windows, and he parted the slats to peer out into the alley. Steel bars covered the outer windows.

Stephanie said: "By the way, what did you pick up out there, in the living room?"

He looked blank for a moment, then searched his pockets for the scrap of celluloid he had found in front of the fireplace. Stephanie bent her head to study it as he held it under the light.

"That's a piece of microfilm," she said. "But where would microfilm come from?"

"I wish I knew," he told her. "But I'm going to hide it good." He considered his wallet, then slid the half-inch triangle securely into his sock, grinned at the girl. "A dame named Mame taught me that. In case I get slugged and this is missing, I'll know you did it."

"Do you expect to get slugged?" she asked.

"You never know."

He began to tinker with the simple ward lock on the closet door. After a moment, with the aid of a narrow automatic pencil, he got the latch to snick aside.

"You're quite an expert," the girl said.

"I told you how I feel about closets. Watch the door."

She moved obediently back to the

hall entrance and leaned against the wall. Blocking the girl's view, Jerry looked into the dim recess of the closet. He stood still for a long moment — for so long that the girl said queerly:

"What's the matter?"

He straightened abruptly, kept his back to the open closet as he faced the girl. He looked shocked and confused. A little muscle wriggled along the ridge of his taut jaw.

"No brandy?" asked the girl.

"No. I think it's Mr. Gantredi."

"Who?"

"Gantredi is in. He's been in, all the time."

The girl's hand went to her mouth. Over her trembling fingers, her eyes were wide and enormous. The apartment was suddenly very quiet. There was only the chill, sullen patter of rain on the windows, the rattle of water in the drainage gutter to the alley.

"*Dead?*" the girl whispered.

"Look for yourself," he said quietly.

5

THE man in the closet was middle-aged, with curly black hair and a little spit-and-polish moustache over a rosebud mouth. He was huddled like a potato sack in a corner of the closet, his knees drawn up to his chin, his round moon face vague and slack in the shadows. His open eyes glittered. There was a dull red stain over his flowered pocket handkerchief, and the wooden handle of a dagger stuck out slantwise from his chest.

The girl leaned forward, her hand trembling on Jerry's arm. She made a queer little sound in her throat.

"It's Gantredi, all right," she whispered.

"How can you tell?" Jerry asked.

"Why, I — I've seen him before. I know him."

"Then this isn't your first visit here?"

The girl's eyes were filled with horror. "You can take my word for it," she said quietly. "That's Gantredi."

"All right," Jerry said. He turned her away with rough hands. "Go to the door and keep the others out of here."

He gave her a little push, away from the closet. She moved slowly away, then turned and watched him with wide, somber eyes while he searched the dead man's pockets. He found several letters addressed to George Gantredi, a pad of rent receipts, and an unmailed letter to the Guarantee Trust Company with Gantredi's signature on it in crabbed, European-style script. The dead man's wallet contained two ten-dollar bills and several singles. A diamond that was probably not a diamond winked in his necktie.

The girl watched Jerry with shocked eyes as he took two of the blank rent receipts and the letter addressed to the bank, with the dead man's signature on it, then frowned and added the dead man's fountain pen to his handful. Sliding the rest back carefully, he closed and locked the closet door.

The girl said queerly: "He's been murdered, of course. Are you going to call the police?"

"Not yet."

"But we must," she whispered. "It's got to be done."

"We want this apartment, don't we?" Jerry asked.

The girl's eyebrows became winged with incredulity. She looked shocked. "But — murder!"

Jerry said: "Use your head, Miss Farley. If we call the cops, they'll seal up this apartment during the investigation, which means a week, at least. On the other hand, if we keep it quiet for twenty minutes, I can fix it so we can move in."

Her voice lowered with suspicion. "How do you mean — we?"

"We'll settle that between ourselves, later. The thing is, we've got to get rid of the others and establish residence.

Then it won't matter, when the cops come. We'll still have the place, between us. Or one of us will, anyway."

"You act as if you find bodies in closets every day."

"Only on alternate Thursdays," Jerry told her.

She shivered and caught her underlip between white teeth.

"Please," he said, "just give me a few minutes. I'll have to go out to fix things. I'll explain it all later."

"I'm scared," she said. "I won't stay here alone."

He studied her. "Too scared?"

"No." She shook her head, her dark hair trembling in sleek waves about her shoulders. "I guess I'm not too scared."

"Good girl." Jerry found his hat on the red couch where he had dropped it, and put it on. "Keep the others out of here as long as you can. And don't say anything to them."

"I won't," she said.

The other prospective tenants were still gathered in the living room when Jerry Benedict left. Nobody paid any attention to him when he turned into the lobby. Mr. and Mrs. Holovacs, of High Corners, Kansas, seemed to have permanently disappeared.

The rain felt colder as he paused on the sidewalk. He remembered a taproom around the corner and set his sights for it, turning up his coat collar as he splashed across the dark cobblestones. A green neon sign advertising Ernie's Bar blinked in the windy darkness. Inside, it was warm and smoky, with the decor of an old English pub. A fat man was squeezed behind one of the round tables in the back, talking to a big-bosomed blonde. Two younger men stood at the bar. One of them was drinking crème de cocoa from a tiny glass. He spoke in a highpitched voice:

"Anyway, that's what I told Arthur. For fifty, or nothing. Otherwise he could take his proposition and stick it."

The other young man looked delighted. "That's what I'd have told him, Hi. You were perfectly right."

The fat man and the big blonde at the rear table glanced up as Jerry came in. The Fat man said something in a Slavic tongue. Jerry passed the barman and said, "Draw one," and stepped into a telephone booth to call the *Globe*.

"Get me McConaughy," he said.

A bored voice said: "Just like that, chum?"

Jerry said: "Go rassle a tassel, Shorty. This is Benedict."

"Oh. Just a second, Jerry."

From the booth he watched the barman fill a tall glass of beer, while he waited. Then McConaughy's burly voice was saying:

"All right, Jerry. Tillie Adams told me what you were up to, and I don't like it. I told you what the boss said about your getting tangled up in this. I know how you feel, but — " The fat man couldn't conceal his curiosity.

"Did you get the apartment?"

"Not yet," Jerry said. "But I think I will. I may have to take a girl along in the deal, but I'll get the apartment."

McConaughy's voice was creamed with sarcasm. "You are just a martyr. What does it look like?"

"Nice. A blue-eyed brunette with a temper and butterflies. I've got the butterflies."

Infinite patience came over the wire. "I mean the setup, you clown."

"The hunch was good," Jerry said. He settled himself in the telephone booth and winked at the woman with the fat man, through the glass panel. "Quite a few people showed, all anxious for a crack at that place. Frankie's girl, Wanda Dykes, and George Chalett, the gambler — they seemed annoyed to see each other. And there's a man from Argentina, named Pedro de Ordas."

"You kidding again?" McConaughy warned.

"On my honor," Jerry said. He winked again at the big blonde. "I know the dirty executioner. He was head of the concentration camp you got me out of, Luscious."

McConaughy whistled. "Cuba?"

"It's a small world," Jerry said. "De Ordas didn't recognize me, but I couldn't forget him. A hood from the Argentine, a born muscle man who worked for pay from the reds, until they got a little sick of his blood lust and kicked him out. He took some loot with him, I've heard — refugee money that he's probably trying to invest through Hamilton and the racket mob lay-off money . . . And there's also a little drunk named Finchley — Oliver Finchley, who was once indicted by the S.E.C. and kicked off the Stock Exchange. Also, a couple from Kansas who look too good to be true. Besides these, there's a Mrs. Quarles who lives upstairs. She might know a lot. Check on them all, anyway."

"Got it," said McConaughy. "What about the super?"

"He's dead," Jerry said.

"How's that again?"

"Gantredi is dead. I found him in a closet. Somebody stabbed him, about an hour ago. I put him back in the closet."

There was an appreciative whistle in the receiver.

"Have you called the cops?"

"Not until I get a chance to search the apartment myself. That's what I think everybody is there for — they're all looking for something, and I wish I knew what it is. I locked the door on the body, anyway, and nobody knows it's there."

McConaughy approved. "You're born for it, boy — but you'll have to watch your step with Cy Dulcey. He doesn't like you a bit."

"It's mutual," Jerry said.

"You wouldn't by any chance know who knocked off Gantredi, would you?"

"Hell, I'll call you back," Jerry said, "when I find out."

He stepped from the booth and picked up his beer with a nod to the barman, and carried it to one of the side tables. The blonde with the fat man winked at him. The fat man turned around, his face congested with rage.

"Wise guy?"

Jerry balanced the beer on the palm of his hand. "Your gal's slip is showing. On top," he said.

The big-bosomed blonde adjusted her dress. Her mouth curled. "Play with the pretty boys at the bar."

Jerry carried his beer to a booth table, and sat quietly for a moment, his eyes brooding. The fat man and the woman began to quarrel in fierce undertones. From his pocket, Jerry took one of the blank rent receipts he had found in the dead man's pocket and smoothed it out. He studied Gantredi's signature on the letter he had taken with it, and with the dead man's fountain-pen practiced Gantredi's script with swift, efficient flourishes. When he was satisfied, he wrote out a rent receipt for the Waverly Walk apartment, dated it, forged Gantredi's name to it, and put it away in his pocket.

The fat man and his woman were still arguing. The two boys at the bar were gone. Jerry flipped a coin to the bartender for his beer and went out into the rain again.

Waverly Walk was deserted. Jerry stepped around a parked cab, ignoring the cabbie's suggestion for a fare, and splashed across the cobblestones between the dark buildings. Rain winked on his face as he ducked down the steps into the lobby of Number 16. The silver clock on the wall stood at 7:25. He shook water from his sodden hat, opened his coat, and pushed into the vacant apartment. There was no one around.

"Stephanie?" he called.

The lights were on, and there was a faintly lingering scent of cigarette smoke in the musty air. His voice echoed hollowly through the disheveled rooms, and he felt sudden alarm. He crossed quickly to the hall, then paused as Mrs. Quarles' big figure came out of the darkness of the kitchen. Her face was as wooden as a cigar store Indian's.

"Where is everybody?" Jerry demanded.

"They've all gone."

"Gone? Where?"

Stephanie appeared from behind the big woman's shadow.

"They just drifted off, darling," she explained. She shook her head in a warning gesture, her sleek hair shining on her shoulders. "Did you see Mr. Gantredi, dear?"

Jerry moistened his lips, tasted the beer he had had at Ernie's bar. Mrs. Quarles' eyes were like lacquered plumbs. All the luster in them lay on the surface.

He said: "I ran into Gantredi on the corner — saved me hunting up his house. I paid him a month's rent in advance."

"How nice," said Mrs. Quarles. She looked unperturbed.

Jerry said: "Why, yes. How nice." He handed her the crumpled rent receipt he had forged in the taproom. The tall woman glanced at it and said: "I'm sure you will be very comfortable here. I've already arranged for the linens. Your wife likes the apartment very much."

"My wife?" Jerry asked blankly.

Stephanie said sweetly: "Remember me, darling?"

"How could I forget?" said Jerry. He bowed gallantly.

Mrs. Quarles said: "You can store Mr. Hamilton's things in the cellar tomorrow. Your wife has the keys to the house."

"Of course," said Jerry. "Thank you."

When Mrs. Quarles was gone, Stephanie moved to the giant sunburst mirror in the living room and studied her reflection in it. Her face looked soft and clear in the lamplight. Her blue eyes mocked Jerry's anger as he stood behind her.

"So now I have a wife," he said grimly.

"Don't take it so hard," she smiled. "If you look more tragic, I'll really be insulted." She finished touching her mouth with lipstick. "You don't think I'd give you a chance to doublecross me out of this apartment, do you? I really do need a place to live, you know — besides everything else."

"What everything else?"

"I mean to have this place — corpses or no corpses. But don't worry," she added. "You can sleep on the couch here."

Jerry said: "That's what you think!"

"Oh?"

"It was your idea, beautiful." He swung her around and tried to kiss her, but she managed to slip aside and he felt quite foolish as he kissed the tip of her left ear. She pulled away from him, her eyes suddenly alarmed.

"Don't be such a stinker," she breathed.

"I'm always ready to take advantage of girls who try to compromise me," Jerry grinned. The girl took another step away from him. "Maybe you'll change your mind a little later on."

"In a pig's eye," she said.

"All right. But tell me — what happened here? Why did everybody disappear?" Jerry surveyed the disheveled living room with distaste, sniffed at the memory of Wanda Dykes' magnolia perfume. "How come they all ran off? I thought they were all pretty anxious to get this place."

"They were anxious enough." She watched him as he prowled restlessly about the room, peering into closets and up the dark, sooty fireplace. "They simply drifted off after you left."

"All together?"

"No," Stephanie said. "First Mr. Finchley decided to call his wife, then that handsome George Chalett went next."

"He's not so handsome," Jerry said.

"It's a matter of opinion. The Duchess picked herself up and tinkle-tinkled the blazes out of here, as if somebody had stuck a pin in her. Come to think of it, I wish I had."

Jerry's voice was muffled as he got down on his hands and knees and examined the baseboard of the opposite wall.

"That Wanda Dykes," he said admiringly. "There's a woman for you. A beautiful beast."

"If you like them like that," Stephanie said coldly.

"Maybe I do. It's a matter of opinion," Jerry said. "What about our South American friend?"

"Señor de Ordas went out with your beast. As far as I know, they didn't find the body. I made sure of that."

Jerry dusted his hands. "But something scared them away."

The girl moved back in front of the mirror again. Her back was straight and

72

arrogant as Jerry studied her. When he raised his eyes, he caught her watching him in the mirror.

"I can't figure Gantredi's death at all," he said. "I don't think he was mixed up in Frank Hamilton's business. But all those other people want something that's in this apartment."

"Like what?" Stephanie asked.

"I don't know. They weren't just looking for a place to live. Whatever is here, they want it badly. Maybe Gantredi found it, and was killed for it. It was an impromptu murder, anyway. The dagger that killed him came from that sunburst mirror you're preening yourself in."

"I'm not preening," said the girl. She frowned at the mirror. "I don't see anything wrong with it."

"When we first came in here," Jerry said, "one of the rays in the frame was missing. It was still missing when I went out just before. Any one of those spikes would make a lethal dagger."

The girl stepped back for a wider

view of the mirror.

"I don't see any missing rays," she said.

Jerry drew her aside suddenly to study the big glass for himself. He counted the golden spikes in the symmetrical frame. There were no gaps anywhere. There were sixteen spikes, and the one that had been missing was replaced.

"That's a fine thing," he said.

He stepped around the girl, reached up, and tried to unscrew one of the spikes, but it was impossible to turn. He closed his eyes for a moment, visualizing the mirror as he had first seen it, then chose a ray close to the bottom of the glass. The razor-edged prism failed to turn when he twisted. Instead, there came a snapping sound and the thing fell away from its socket in the heavy frame. Jerry fingered the circular hole, more than an inch in diameter. His fingernail caught on something and he worked carefully for a moment, extracting it.

"It was another scrap of dark celluloid.

Stephanie whispered: "More micro-film?"

Jerry nodded. "Looks like there was a whole roll of it in here. Somebody got away with all but this bit that snagged."

He turned his attention to the metal ray, after dropping the second piece of film into his sock. The handle of the spike was almost four inches long. He held it under a table lamp and studied the makeshift dagger.

"Are those blood spots?" Stephanie asked quietly.

Jerry nodded, puzzled. "And somebody put this thing back where it belongs. Plenty peculiar." He stood with his back to the mirror and raised both hands experimentally, as if he was covered by a gun. His right hand came several inches above the gaping socket in the mirror frame. He frowned. "Two possibilities. Either somebody grabbed it by accident, or already knew about it. In either case, he killed Gantredi with it, then took it from Gantredi's body while I was out and — "

He suddenly spun on his heel toward the door.

"Come on!" he rapped.

The closet door in the study was still locked, and he cursed with impatience as he picked the latch again. But there was no need to hurry. The closet was empty.

Mr. Gantredi's body was gone.

6

STEPHANIE looked blank. "Maybe he wasn't dead in the first place. Maybe he just got up and walked away."

They were in the kitchen. She was standing on tiptoe to investigate the pantry shelves. Jerry sat with folded arms over the back of a green kitchen chair and watched her. She seemed totally absorbed in her task of investigating the cupboards. He sighed and rubbed his chin on his arm, and the girl looked at him over her shoulder.

"After all," she said, "funnier things than that have happened. You're not a doctor, are you? Maybe he really wasn't dead."

"I touched him," Jerry said. "He was dead, all right. And somebody moved his body and put the spike back into the mirror frame. It was a fast, neat job — and it was done right under your nose." He regarded her with suspicion.

Stephanie didn't seem to hear. She was examining the contents of a carton of eggs she found in the icebox.

"They're stale," Jerry said impatiently. "Listen to me. The body can't be too far away. It may still be in this very apartment. How long were you in the study while I was gone?"

"Oh, I was in and out. We all went into the lobby after you left. Mrs. Quarles insisted. Any one of them could have gone back, though, because they were wandering all over the place, all the time."

"And then they just drifted out?"

"Yes, one by one, as I told you."

"Nobody seemed alarmed?"

"None of them — except your gorgeous Wanda. She lit out as if a bee had stung her." Stephanie paused and looked at Jerry's angular figure. "Now that the body is gone, do you think we should still call the police?"

"Not yet." He looked with sudden exasperation as she lit the stove and deftly cracked six eggs into the frying pan, together with a slice of ham she had found in the icebox. "Look, you dumb bunny, that food has been here at least two weeks. Don't plan to get rid of me by ptomaine."

Stephanie said: "You may be smart, but you're not a cook. I'm starved, and this food is fresh — almost as fresh as you are, Mr. Benedict. Somebody has been living in this apartment in between police visits, and no later than yesterday too."

"Are you sure?" Jerry came out of the chair like a jack-in-the-box. Sudden interest wiped the restiveness from his eyes. He said admiringly: "You know, you should be a detective."

"Is that what you are?" she asked.

"Don't even suggest it," he said shortly.

"Then what are you?"

"Just a guy trying to get along." He admired the pan of ham and eggs,

79

frying under the girl's expert touch. "Cooking is always an asset in a wife, although it isn't a prime requisite. They say a good wife should be an expert cook in the kitchen, a little lady in the parlor, and a mistress in the bedroom, Miss Farley."

"You're taking that marriage business too seriously," she said. "But you can call me Steve."

"All right," he said. "It's Steve."

"Is it just the food that's making you behave so nicely?"

"I want to call a truce," he suggested. "That's all."

"That suits me," she smiled.

He wondered how she could look so lovely, when he was quite convinced that she was an efficient liar. He was aware of a cool antagonism in her, a determination on her part not to give him any more help than was necessary to maintain her pose. It was as if she were strengthened by some knowledge of facts as yet unknown to him; as if she were merely standing by in the breach, confidently waiting for someone or something to take the problem off her shoulders.

Annoyed, he began searching through the apartment again, wandering from room to room. There was plenty of evidence to indicate that Frank Hamilton had left without any warning — or with every intention of a prompt return. There were all his clothes, a battery of hair tonics, shaving lotions, and bottles of masculine perfume, monogrammed with Frank Hamilton's initials. In a tray on the bureau were assorted golden hairpins, a woman's nail buffer, and a squat jar of cold cream. Jerry frowned, chewed a fingernail, and opened the dresser drawers. One of the top drawers was entirely devoted to feminine lingerie. In the tall wardrobe chest were more monogrammed dressing gowns, several negligées, a baby blue slip, and pink, fluffy mules.

"What-a-man Frankie," he muttered.

There were four toothbrushes in the bathroom and another battery of feminine beauty aids mingled with Hamilton's ebony-and-gold shaving gear. Nobody was hiding in the shower stall. The bathroom window opened on the same small alleyway, and he bumped his head sharply on the window bars when he tried to look out. Blustery rain dashed into his face as he peered into the dark passageway. There were no dead men hidden in the alley.

From the dining room a doorway opened into a rickety flight of wooden stairs that zigzagged down into deep darkness. He groped for the light switch and clicked it several times, futilely. The cellar remained in brooding darkness. Carefully, he locked the cellar door and returned to the kitchen.

Stephanie had just finished setting the table.

"Find anything?" she asked.

"I'll need a flashlight."

"There are some candles in the cupboard. But sit down and eat first. I'm famished."

She had found some cans of beer and

poured the brew into tall tumblers. He liked the way she moved her hands. They were good hands, with long sensitive fingers. Absently, he took a pad of paper from his pocket and began sketching in deft, quick strokes. To Jerry, caricatures were a form of doodling. Finished one, he flipped the page and began another, frowning.

He noticed that Stephanie wore no rings except a small amethyst on her little finger. Her gray dress was simple but expensive, and he wondered about it until he remembered that she was a model, and models invest most of their income in wardrobes. But she would look good in anything, he decided.

"How are you mixed up in all this?" she asked quietly.

"I'm not really mixed up in it," he said. He tried the ham and eggs, and found it good. "I'm sure you know a lot more about it than I. But if you don't trust me, we'll just go on pretending." He tried the beer, and that was good, too. "Frank Hamilton made his start in the brave early thirties, in bootleg liquor, driving a truck when he was sixteen. Later he went into politics — a natural step — and I guess he was as honest as some of our state senators. But there was a scandal about the drug racket controls, and he sort of retired through the war years. Then he tried the new rackets. Guess he couldn't resist temptation."

"Black markets," Stephanie murmured. "It seems that no one has a good word for Hamilton, even now, when he's dead."

Jerry's mouth tightened. "Narcotics and black markets certainly flourished under Frank Hamilton's expert touch. But when the Internal Revenue people got close to him, he turned legit and became known as 'The Investor' for the mobs, for the overflow of gambling money from Vegas, the rackets in dope and numbers — you name it. He put this cash into apartment houses, stocks and bonds, legitimate manufacturing companies, as a cover for the Cosa

Nostra profits. But the government was getting close to him. He stood to face a long stretch, and was threatened with an indictment any day. He offered to sing, in the hope of a lenient sentence."

"And then he disappeared?"

Jerry nodded. "The police watched him night and day, but he vanished just the same. A few days later they called in Wanda Dykes, Frankie's inamorata, to identify a body they fished out of the North River. To make doubly sure, they also grilled another feminine visitor to this house. Both girls sobbed prettily into their hankies and said yes, it was poor Francis." Jerry met the girl's cool stare. "Anyway, Dulcey tagged the corpse, but not where they usually do, on the big toe, because this body didn't have a leg to stand on, let alone two feet."

"I know," Stephanie whispered.

"Hamilton had a club foot," Jerry went on, "but both legs of this body were gone at the knees. That struck me as a happy coincidence. Made it easy to palm off this stiff as Frank Hamilton. I checked on the whereabouts of one of his associates, a Johnny Lisbon, but by another coincidence, Lisbon had also disappeared. So I got Lisbon's girl, Patti Duggan, into Dulcey's office this afternoon and showed her the pictures of the corpse. And she fainted."

Stephanie's mouth trembled. "It *wasn't* Frank Hamilton?"

"She said it was Johnny Lisbon. My editor gave me until tomorrow morning to look into it."

Stephanie still looked calm, but something shimmered in her wide eyes.

"Then you're a newspaper man," she said. She reached over the table and took Jerry's scratch pad, looked at the deft little caricatures he had drawn. "Why, that's me! And this one with the long face — he looks like Mephistopheles, doesn't he? — that's Señor de Ordas! And George Chalett!" She laughed, suddenly pleased. "You're

Jerry Benedict — the cartoonist!"

"Guilty," he nodded. "And you?"

She swallowed. "Nobody."

Jerry said gently: "Look, honey, I'm on your side, although I don't know why. I wish you would trust me."

She shook her head. "There's no great mystery about me. When I came to New York last year, I had a letter to Hamilton from a mutual friend, and he helped me get started as a model. We didn't see much of each other, although I dropped in every now and then, and the last time was when the police were here, that's all. They seemed to think I knew where Frank was. So did Frank's friends, until the police found that body. Then George Chalett came to my place and told me to be sure to identify the body as Mr. Hamilton's."

"Even if it didn't turn out to be Frank?" Jerry asked.

"That's right."

"And after Dulcey called you down to headquarters, you knew it wasn't 'The Investor'?"

"I really couldn't tell," said Stephanie impatiently. "Chalett frightened me." Her blue eyes went dark with the remembrance of fear. "Chalett said something awful would happen to me if I — if I didn't do what I was told."

Jerry snorted. "That George! I thought you said he was so handsome."

"I was only trying to annoy you."

"Well, I am annoyed," Jerry said. He took a deep breath. "Did Chalett send you here to rent the apartment, too?"

"No, that was my own idea," Steve said. "I thought I might find out what happened to Hamilton this way. Whatever everybody else thinks of him, he helped me tremendously when I first came to New York, and was very kind. I thought I owed it to him, to try to learn what had happened here."

He said suddenly: "Do you think Hamilton is still alive?"

"I'm sure of it." There was a sudden challenging lift to her chin. "Whatever happened here, he'll be back and straighten it all out." She looked puzzled for a moment. "I just don't understand what all these people want here, though. Do you?"

Jerry said: "Not yet. But all of Hamilton's old buddies seem mighty anxious to move in. I thought you might be one of them. Or working with them, anyway."

Stephanie tossed her head. "Did you classify me with Wanda Dykes?"

"That was before you and I got married," Jerry grinned.

"Don't let that go to your head," she warned.

"But now that we're old married folks . . . "

Without warning, all the lights went out.

7

THE sudden plunge into darkness was stifling. Jerry sat still, stiffening in his chair at the kitchen table. The rain sounded abnormally loud in the abrupt stillness. From out of the dark came Stephanie's voice, sharply suspicious.

"How convenient. Did you arrange this, Galahad?"

Jerry said tightly: "Keep quiet."

"I — "

"Shut up!" he said.

Stephanie shut up. Through the darkness advanced the drumming, lulling patter of rain on the cobblestones outside. Jerry squeezed his eyes shut, then opened them again. He could make out the dim rectangle of the kitchen window, and the faintest patch of pallor where the girl's face floated opposite him, across the table. He slid his chair back carefully, and the girl whispered in sudden panic: "Is that you, Jerry?" He said: "For God's sake, be still." Crossing to the cupboard, he fumbled for the candles on the second shelf. He struck a match, and the flare was like a tiny sun in the darkness. The kitchen wavered back into existence. The girl was still sitting at the table, her face pale.

"Was it a fuse?" she whispered.

"Maybe not." He let the candle drip on the procelain table, fastened it there in the molten wax, and lit another. "I'm going to look around."

"And leave me here?" she asked dubiously.

"You invited yourself to the party," he told her. Then he saw the real anxiety in her eyes. From his trenchcoat he took a small .32 Colt and put it in her hand. Her eyes widened for a moment; her fingers felt cool and smooth on his wrist. He said warningly: "Don't let anybody in while I'm gone."

"Can't I go with you?" she asked.

"I'd be scared stiff all alone."

"You'd better stay put."

Holding the candle in one hand, he moved soundlessly toward the living room. The house was wrapped in dark silence. At the lobby door he looked back and saw that Steve had followed him. She stood in the kitchen hallway, holding the candle aloft in one hand, the gun in the other.

"Jerry," she called. "Wait a minute."

She moved quickly across the living room to the sunburst mirror over the fireplace. The candle in her hand sputtered and dripped wax on the floor. In the flickering light she looked lovelier than ever. Her eyes were dark with anxiety.

"Look," she said. "Someone was in here just now."

"I see it," he said.

The golden symmetry of the mirror frame was oddly awry. The spike that killed Gantredi was missing again. The socket gaped like a missing tooth in the heavy frame.

"Did you take it just now?" the girl whispered.

"*I?*"

"Well, *I* didn't," the girl said.

Jerry felt his mouth grow dry.

"Can you handle that gun?" he asked.

"I think so."

"Don't let anybody come near you," he said. "And lock the door after me."

"All right," she nodded.

He eased the door open and stepped into the outer lobby. It was dark here, as it was in the apartment; apparently a master fuse had been blown. Enough light filtered through from the street to outline the stairs to the second floor. He closed the apartment door behind him, turning his head as he did so. When he looked back at the dim staircase he thought he saw something move on the landing. What had caught his eye was the movement itself, rather than the person or thing crouching there.

Another sound caught his attention

for a moment. A shoe scuffed on the street steps, then the door opened with a swift hissing of pneumatic stops and a man came awkwardly down the three steps to the lobby. A gust of wind made the candle in Jerry's hand flicker and almost go out. He shielded it with one hand and crossed the dimness to where the man stood shaking rain from his coat.

It was the elfish Mr. Oliver Finchley, Incorporated. He looked as if he had been walking in the rain for a long time. He peered around Jerry, as if seeking something, and then giggled in his high, flutey voice.

"Whassa matter with the lights?"

"They won't work," said Jerry. "What are you doing here?"

"It's my wife. Horrible woman." Mr. Finchley shuddered emphatically. "She says I am strunk — I am drunk. She locked me out."

"What did you come back here for?"

The little man sighed wearily, said: "I came to moo Worpheus."

He sat down with drunken suddenness on the bench against the wall, put his head back, and promptly began to snore. Jerry watched him for a moment, then turned and went quickly up the stairs to the lower landing.

No one was there.

Beyond the flickering radius of the candle glow, the upper hallway was in deep darkness. A sprig of pussywillow stood in a white vase near the head of the stairs. The door nearby had a card in a small brass bracket, reading: *Lucy Quarles, R.N.* Jerry lifted his brows in mild surprise, considered the violet, square librarian's script, and turned down the hall, vaguely aware of something missing in the corridor, but unable to decide just what it was. The door in the wall at the opposite end of the hall was firmly locked. If anyone had come up here, he had vanished behind one of the two doors — and taken the dagger-spike with him.

He went back and rang Mrs. Quarles' bell.

Somewhere beyond the door a bell pealed shrilly. He waited a moment, then rang again. The door opened and Mrs. Quarles filled the entrance. She had changed her clothes. She looked mountainous in a faded, mouse-gray flannel bathrobe; but her hair was still piled in thick, neat coils on top of her head. Her broad, flat-cheeked face was impassive; her eyes were just eyes, looking first at the candle, then at Jerry's tall figure. There was no light in the rooms behind her.

"Did you ring?" she asked. "The lights seem to have gone out. I'd better check the fuses for you."

She made no move to invite him into her apartment. Her figure suggested a roadblock that could only be removed by a generous charge of dynamite. Jerry said: "Did anyone come in here just now, Mrs. Quarles?"

"I told you, young man, I was asleep."

"But it's only a little after eight," he objected.

Mrs. Quarles might have been annoyed: Jerry couldn't quite interpret the vague flicker of emotion that crossed her inscrutable face. She said: "I live a strenuous physical life, Mr. Benedict. I am an athletic instructor and a masseuse, eight hours a day, seven days a week, and I am not as young as I once was. I always retire early."

Jerry said: "You should stay awake a little longer now and then, Mrs. Quarles. There's something odd going on here."

"I don't doubt it," the big woman said briefly.

Jerry felt vaguely at a loss. "Then if you're aware of what's been happening — "

"I am only aware of the fact that you and your wife behave rather oddly for a newly married couple," Mrs. Quarles said evenly.

Jerry tried to look shy, and knew he only looked foolish.

"You know how it is with newlyweds,"

he said, and winked.

"You needn't be impertinent, young man."

"I wasn't," he said hastily. "Anyway, somebody deliberately blew the fuses, I think, and then came snooping into our apartment. My wife was quite distressed, as you can imagine. I followed him up here, but he seems to have disappeared."

"He?"

"Well, it could have been a woman, at that."

"More likely, it was your imagination," said Mrs. Quarles.

Jerry thought of the missing dagger. "I'm afraid not." He pointed down the hall to the closed door at the end. "Where does that lead to?"

"Nowhere," said Mrs. Quarles.

"It's got to go somewhere," Jerry insisted. He felt as if he were trying to move a mountain. "Is it a closet?"

The big woman hesitated, said: "It goes to the third floor apartment, but that door is locked and never used."

"The third floor?" Jerry was astonished. Of course, the house had three floors; all the houses on Waverly Walk had three floors. The thing that had puzzled him when he first came upstairs was clear now. He said: "Who lives upstairs, above you?"

"A Mr. Julian Street." Mrs. Quarles adjusted her flannel bathrobe more firmly across her massive bosom. "Mr. Street is a recluse, a retired artist, and perhaps a bit eccentric. He had the back stairway shut off permanently from the rest of the house by that interior door."

"Then how does he get in or out?"

"He uses the outside stairway in the back, which amounts to a private entrance, from Harvey Street, around the corner. His mail comes to that address, too."

"What does he look like?" Jerry asked.

"I don't know, I'm sure. I've never seen him."

"How long has he been living here?"

"Several months." Mrs. Quarles looked at the guttering candle in Jerry's fingers. "I'll get a flashlight you can use to light your way around, until I replace the fuse in the cellar."

The door closed sharply in his face, leaving him alone in the hall. Returning Mrs. Quarles reopened it just wide enough to hand him a small pocket torch. He tested it, blew out the candle, and said: "Thank you. About Mr. Street — "

The door slammed shut. Shrugging, Jerry turned to the end of the corridor and the door blocking off the third-floor apartment.

But it was firmly locked.

8

JERRY frowned, rubbed an index finger around the glass knob. There was no dust on his finger. He went down to the lobby again after a moment, employing the pocket torch to guide his steps. Finchley was still on the bench, snoring lightly. He looked more than ever like an elf, with his enormous pointed ears and round, gently perspiring face.

It had stopped raining, and the cobblestones on deserted Waverly Walk were shiny and black. Pools of water winked placidly in the feeble glow of the Colonial street lamp, and only a few windows in the adjacent houses were alight. Jerry's heels echoed hollowly as he turned toward Harvey Street.

His thoughts were full of Stephanie Farley. Not for a moment did he accept the story of her vague connection with

Frank Hamilton. On the other hand, she didn't fit into the picture as Wanda Dykes did.

A small crowd was gathered at the entrance to Ernie's Bar. A uniformed cop was saying mildly, "Now, folks, break it up, please. The show is over. Go on home and get dried out." Nobody paid any attention to him.

The cab was still parked two doors beyond the taproom. Jerry crossed the street and touched the driver's arm. The cabby yawned and said, "You want to go somewhere, Mack?"

Jerry shook his head. "What's the trouble?"

"Fellow beat up his wife in Ernie's," the cabby said. "Started just after you left."

"A fat fellow and a big blonde?" Jerry asked.

"That's them. It happens all the time."

Jerry returned to Harvey Street. By counting off the houses, he soon reached the back of what was Number 16 on the other side of the block. A small alleyway ran between a liquor store and a pet shop, ending in a blank door. The liquor store was closed, but the pet shop was lighted, and a bald little man was puttering among some parrot cages. A little bell jangled nervously over Jerry's head as he went inside, and the bald man came hurrying forward, wiping his hands on a white apron.

"Yes, sir? What can I do for you?"

The parrot in the nearest cage squawked: "Maisie, goddamit, I'm telling you for the last time!" There were round-eyed goldfish in a huge aquarium and a marmoset assiduously searching for wild life on his hairy little chest.

"I'm looking for a Mr. Julian Street," Jerry said.

"Oh. You don't want to buy anything? No bird seed?"

"No bird seed. Just Mr. Street."

The bald man turned to the squawking parrot and said: "Why don't you shut up?" The parrot cursed angrily. The petshop man said: "I'm closing up, mister."

"But he lives around here. Next door, I think."

"Well, go next door, then."

"There's nobody home. I just wondered — "

The bald man said: "I don't know him very well. As a matter of fact, I've never even seen him."

"But he lives next door?" Jerry insisted.

"Oh, my, yes. I was talking to the mailman about Mr. Street just the other day, because nobody's ever seen him."

"Doesn't he ever have any visitors?"

"Sometimes." The bald man squinted into Jerry's face. "Are you a bill-collector, or something?"

"Just a friend," Jerry said. "So he gets a lot of visitors?"

"I didn't say that. Don't go putting words in my mouth, young man. I just said he has visitors sometimes, that's all. Good night."

The parrot shrieked: "You're just a jerk! Good-night!"

Jerry said: "Well, thanks, anyway."

The bell jangled over his head again as he closed the door. The wind whimpered in the alley between the pet shop and liquor store. The rain had failed to penetrate to the small stoop, sheltered by a small ornamental entablature, but where the bricks were dry his flashlight showed several wet patches that might have been recent footprints. There seemed to be two sets of prints, one large, and the other quite small, but they had no shape at all.

There was no name over the bell. The door had a brass lever handle and Jerry tried it with care, felt the latch snick aside. It wasn't locked. Pushing the door inward with his fingertips, he sprayed light up a steep shaft of stairs. The stairs proceeded directly to the third-floor landing, without a break. On the third floor he turned off his flashlight and tested the door carefully.

Like the street door, this one wasn't locked either.

There was only darkness before him.

He tried his torch, saw only a short foyer and an arch into a living room. In silence, he went inside and began searching the dark, quiet apartment.

There was a wood-burning fireplace in the living room, which would have been ordinary enough, with its furniture of department store bargain variety, except that all the upholstering had been slashed and ripped to ribbons as if by some berserk, tusked animal. The rug had been picked up and hurled aside, helter-skelter; the window blinds were hauled all the way down, exposing the wooden roller. An imitation Queen Anne chair lay on its back, one leg broken off, A Governor Winthrop secretary stood in a Georgian niche with all its drawers open and empty. Papers lay in a snowdrift against the wall baseboard.

The closets were empty. The ash trays held only dust. In the kitchen cupboards there were no dishes, except for half a dozen sticky tumblers on the washboard of the sink. The refrigerator was warm, the plug pulled out. In the bathroom, Jerry found a safety-razor, two dirty towels, a dry, cracked cake of soap, and a packet of Band-Aid. There was an empty liquor bottle on the toilet box, another quart bottle of ginger-ale, also empty, on the tile floor of the shower stall. Dust grayed the bottom of the bath-tub.

Frowning, he turned his torch back to the bathroom door — and suddenly froze in mid-step, his flashlight steady on the pebbled glass door.

The dark imprint of a man's hand showed on the opaque panel. Jerry felt his throat tighten, then he stepped forward to touch the palm print with cautious fingers. It was almost dry; it felt cool and gummy under his fingertip. He went, almost frantically, into the last room, the bedroom.

The mattress frame was half flung to the floor, revealing dusty coil springs on the slats. A man sprawled on his back on the twisted bed, his arms outflung, his face turned up to the ceiling. His eyes stared unwinkingly into the glare of Jerry's torch; the pupils glistened like glass marbles.

Jerry had never seen him before.

It wasn't Mr. Gantredi.

But he was just as dead.

He had been tall and heavy set, about fifty, with smooth, cotton-white hair, dark eyebrows, and a clipped military moustache that was dark against the pallor of his dead face. His clothes looked too tight on his big frame, as if they didn't belong to him. The white shirt collar was open, and he had no necktie. Half of his head was covered with a neat surgical bandage, as if he had recently suffered a skull injury. But sticking out of his chest was the familiar shaft of the sunburst spike. There wasn't much blood.

A white silk scarf lay on the floor near the dead man's dangling feet. Jerry picked it up, became aware of perfume, and sniffed it cautiously. An odd look came into his eyes. Turning back to the dead man, he went carefully through all the pockets of the ill-fitting suit. The pockets were empty. There was nothing whatever to identify him, but he presumed the dead man to be Mr. Julian Street.

Returning to the living room, Jerry set the flashlight on the table and picked up the telephone. He noted the number — Waldorf 9-6656 — while he dialed the *Globe*. It seemed vaguely familiar.

It started to rain again while he waited: soft pattering drops that tinkled on the dark window panes. The apartment felt airless, too warm for comfort. He thought about the dead man lying on his back with a sun ray in his heart, and made a wry face in the gloom.

McConaughy's voice cracked tinnily in his ear.

"It's about time, Jerry. What's been going on?"

Jerry said crisply: "First of all, somebody swiped Gantredi's body while I was out calling you the last time, and I haven't found it yet. Everybody else took a powder, too. And now I've got another stiff on my hands."

"*Another* stiff?" McConaughy's voice slid up the scale. "Not Gantredi?"

"No, not Gantredi."

"Well, who is it?"

"I don't know everything, Lucius. Give me a chance."

"What about the police?"

"Leave them out just now," Jerry said. "I've got troubles enough. That is, if it won't bounce."

"It will bounce plenty, but that's a chance we'll take."

"I like that '*we*' spirit," Jerry said disgustedly.

"We'll back you to the hilt, boy," McConaughy said. Jerry thought it was an unfortunate figure of speech. He listened to the editor go on. "Dulcey will play merry hell if he finds you're

110

covering two corpses, though. I'd like to see his face, all right, and that's a fact. That will be a good one."

"Go ahead and laugh," Jerry said. "Choke on it."

"Well, listen — I've done some checking for you. That Holovacs couple is registered at the St. Martin, from Kansas, sure enough. Bona-fide. Wanda Dykes lives at the Regent, and she hasn't been seen all day. Neither has George Chalett."

"What about Finchley?" Jerry asked.

"He's president of Allied Food Distributors, Incorporated — might be a tieup there to Hamilton's gangland investment activities. As for Señor de Ordas — I guess you were right about him. He's posing as a financial genius sent up here from Argentina to discuss a loan. The consulate acts as if they're suspicious of him. They went into a tizzy when I started asking questions. I think it's got to be hands off him; he's too touchy."

"The hell," Jerry said. "You don't

keep hands off a war criminal like that . . . What about Mrs. Quarles?"

"I'm checking her now. She's difficult to trace — was on the stage, long ago, and used a lot of names. She's a registered nurse now, working for a Dr. Polders here in town."

Jerry said: "Listen, when Hamilton disappeared, the cops went through all his stuff, didn't they?"

"All they could find, but there wasn't anything in it. Why?"

"There's a safe in the study closet. I was wondering."

McConaughy said: "There won't be anything in it that Dulcey hasn't already seen. You won't find anything in an obvious place, Jerry, or those others would have had it by now. Maybe they have, already."

Jerry said: "Not with this second stiff still warm. He was killed only half an hour ago, and whatever it is that's going on around here hasn't come to an end yet."

Anxiety crept into the other's voice.

"Maybe you'd better pull out then, Jerry. We could run the story on what we have. If there's a killer loose around there, I don't like keeping you on the scene . . . "

"I can handle it for a while," Jerry said. "I'll ring you again. There's a funny setup I just stumbled into. I'm calling from the third-floor apartment, and it's been searched, just like Hamilton's was, downstairs. The second dead guy is up here. I — "

He broke off suddenly and stood listening.

McConaughy's voice in the receiver said: "Jerry?" He sounded very far away. "Jerry, you still there?"

"I've got company," Jerry whispered. "I'll ring back."

He cradled the phone softly and snapped off the flashlight with a swift movement. The room was plunged into abrupt darkness. Stepping away from the outline of the window, he stood very still, listening.

The sound came from the bedroom,

where he had left the dead man. He hated to think that this one, too, was getting up to walk away. He wished he had the gun he had so chivalrously given to Stephanie Farley. After a moment, when nothing happened, he moved softly through the darkness of the hall and paused under the arch. He couldn't see or hear anything. But there was perfume in the air, thick and cloying, all around him . . .

Something crashed explosively on the back of his head, jolting him to his knees. He twisted, grabbed blindly, his fingers catching on rough cloth. A second blow slammed across his forehead and he flattened on the floor and lay still. He felt as if he were on a pinwheel, spinning around and around. Someone stumbled painfully over his shins, then dim footsteps ran away, toward the door in the back of the hall. The door slammed.

9

LIGHT glaring through his eyelids shocked him back to consciousness. He put his hand to his head and his fingers came away warm and wet. He sat up in sudden alarm.

The electricity was on again. A lamp burned in the living room behind him. It must have been on before the fuse first blew out, he decided.

He got to his feet by clambering up the wall, and his hands left ugly dark smears on the flowered paper. His fingers were covered with blood. He touched his forehead, winced, and discovered the blood was his own.

The light in the bathroom worked, too. He filled the washbowl, cursing monotonously, and plunged his head into cold water. From the medicine cabinet he took the Band-Aid packet and gingerly taped the cut on his forehead. Looking back at the hall, he saw fragments and shards of what had once been a white flower pot. He headed for the bedroom.

The dead man was still there. That was something, anyway. But the spoke that had been thrust into his heart was gone, and that was something else, again.

He stared sharply, then, as his sudden suspicion grew clear, he dropped to one knee and quickly examined the limp feet that dangled over the bed. He had overlooked them before. One of the shoes was heavily built up.

Jerry straightened quickly. The apartment was silent. When he left, he chose the steep flight of steps going down toward the front part of the house. The stairs ended in a door, equipped with a bolt, but it wasn't made fast. When he stepped through, he found himself in the second-floor corridor, with Mrs. Quarles' apartment at the other end.

The white vase that had stood on the table here was gone. The pussy-willow sprigs were neatly piled on the floor at the door.

Mrs. Quarles, still wearing the mousey flannel robe, came up from the lobby when Jerry crossed to her door. She carried a three-cell flashlight in her left hand. Her dark eyes disapproved of him, standing there at her doorway.

"I've just fixed the fuses," she announced. "Somebody removed them all. I put in new ones." She stared at him. "I do not approve of practical jokes, Mr. Benedict."

"It wasn't me," said Jerry. "And I don't think it was a practical joke. I told you there was something funny going on in this house. I'd like to talk to you about it."

She paused with her hand on the doorknob. "All right."

"Inside this time," said Jerry.

Nothing changed in the woman's face. She looked at him for a moment, then shrugged heavily and opened the door.

"What happened to you?" she asked. "Your head is bleeding."

"I ran into something. I'm all right."

"You ran into something," she repeated. "How awkward."

"Quite so," Jerry said.

Every inch of space in her living room was filled with some piece of bric-a-brac, with mountains of silk pillows on the huge studio couch, Victorian tables, dark pie-crust taborets, and a print of the Coliseum and a faded chromo of Despair over the fireplace. There were also several framed photographs, mostly of nude women in various poses of shy sorrow. Mrs. Quarles reversed one promptly as Jerry came in, but not before he caught a glimpse of it. The subject, a girl with a flapper bob of the twenties, seemed to be floating in space, her heavily mascared eyes dreamy and glazed. Jerry couldn't help staring at it.

Mrs. Quarles said quietly: "She was a morphine addict."

"Did you know her?"

"Quite well," said Mrs. Quarles. She hesitated and put the photograph face down on a table, concealing it from Jerry's stare. "As a matter of fact, that's a photograph of myself."

"You?"

"It was taken twenty-five years ago, of course. When I was cured, I dedicated my life to pure, healthful living, regular exercise, and redemption for others."

He felt a little embarrassed, for some obscure reason, and looked around for a place to sit down. Mrs. Quarles pushed aside a lemon silk cushion marked, *Atlantic City, 1927*, in scarlet embroidery.

"I let you in here," she said evenly, "because I like you, young man. I think you and that girl would do well to take my advice."

"You mean my wife?" Jerry asked.

Mrs. Quarles said: "I know you two are not married."

"Jerry said: "How embarrassing."

"It doesn't matter. But I would

suggest that you both leave here as soon as possible. In other words, I suggest that you give up that apartment immediately."

"Just because you think Stephanie and I — "

"I told you, that does not matter. But Mr. Hamilton was a strange and dangerous man, with dangerous friends. The police announcement that they had found his body, cruelly murdered, did not satisfy me. And it is true that strange things are happening here. I am afraid it is too dangerous for you to remain. And of course," she added, "You should not ask for your money back."

"Why not?" Jerry asked. "I paid Mr. Gantredi the rent — "

"I doubt it," Mrs. Quarles said. Her voice was flat. "You see, I've just been to the cellar."

"The cellar?" Jerry had difficulty following her.

"To fix the fuses. I found Mr. Gantredi where you left him."

120

"You found Mr. Gantredi, where *I* left him?"

"In the coal bin. Quite so."

"What did you say?" Jerry asked.

Mrs. Quarles said: "You need not be flippant, young man. We both know that Mr. Gantredi is dead."

Jerry got to his feet.

"I want to make a telephone call," he said. "I want to make it before the police get here. Otherwise I'll be skinned alive for slipping up on this."

Mrs. Quarles was unperturbed. "Sit down. The police aren't coming. I haven't called them yet."

Jerry paused, infinitely relieved. He was beginning to like Mrs. Lucy Quarles. She had possibilities. He watched her broad, inscrutable face in the dull light from a rose-shaded, tasseled lamp, and sat down again among the souvenir cushions.

Mrs. Quarles said: "You're not a regular reporter, are you? You're that cartoonist fellow they say is — always crusading for something or other."

Jerry nodded. "Frankly, my editor and I weren't satisfied about Hamilton's alleged death. We thought Hamilton was alive somewhere, and that a body was palmed off on the police to make it appear as if he were dead and beyond their reach. When the ad appeared about the vacant apartment, I came over to look around. So far, it's worked out fine."

"I can see nothing pleasant in the thought of Frank Hamilton still being alive," said Mrs. Quarles.

"Did you ever see any of the people who were here tonight, before?"

Mrs. Quarles' dark plum eyes took on a faint glitter. "That Dykes woman was here frequently. So was that distinguished-looking Mr. Chalett. Mr. Finchley, who made quite a spectacle of himself, pretending to be drunk, was here often."

"Finchley?" Jerry asked. "Pretending to be drunk?" He thought of the little elf, 'mooing Worpheus,' and felt annoyed. "What about the others?"

"No, I never saw any of them before."

"What about that South American — Señor de Ordas?"

"No," Mrs. Quarles repeated.

Jerry sat forward among the cushions. A hideous African idol, possibly made in Brooklyn, leered up at him from the floor.

"Tell me," he said earnestly. "You leave this house at regular hours, every day, on your job, don't you?"

Mrs. Quarles nodded. "Yes, every day. As I said, I am a health advisor and masseuse. I am employed by Dr. Polders, on West 71st Street. It is a private hospital."

"Then you didn't see Hamilton very often?"

"Only rarely."

"When did you first learn that he was missing?"

"The next day. It was in the papers. I saw Mr. Hamilton only the day before, too." Mrs. Quarles' hands were quiet in her ample lap. "He nodded to me in the lobby, going out."

"And he never came back?"

"Not to my knowledge."

"Was he alone when you saw him last, going out?"

"Quite alone."

"And his apartment has been empty ever since?" Jerry persisted. "Didn't you see anything, or hear anything, going on down there for the past two weeks?"

"I do not pry into affairs of no concern to me."

"What about Gantredi?" Jerry asked. "Do you know who might have killed him?"

"I have several ideas," Mrs. Quarles said.

"Whom do you have in mind?"

Mrs. Quarles said: "You."

"Me?"

"Or that girl."

"Stephanie?"

"Whatever her name is."

"You think she killed Mr. Gantredi?"

"It is quite possible."

"Why, in heaven's name?" Jerry exploded.

"She's been here before, like the others."

"That doesn't prove anything."

"But she had quite a violent quarrel yesterday, with Mr. Gantredi, when he refused to let her have the apartment. She was told to wait until it was properly advertised. She was very anxious to move into this house."

Steam rattled in the radiators, and rain whimpered on the window panes. Jerry said: "Are you going to tell all this to the police?"

"I am," Mrs. Quarles nodded. "I like you, young man. I do not believe that either you or the girl are criminals. That is why I suggest that you leave here at once, before I telephone the authorities about Mr. Gantredi's death."

"Look," Jerry said. "Give me a few minutes before you use that phone."

"If you wish," said Mrs. Quarles. She added, without intending to be funny: "Mr. Gantredi can wait."

He started for the hall door, then, as if in afterthought, he paused and took out the white scarf he had found upstairs, rippling it through his fingers. He put it down on an end table in the foyer.

"I guess this is yours," he said. "I found it outside."

Mrs. Quarles stared blankly. "It is not mine. You know very well it is not mine. It belongs to Miss Wanda Dykes. She was wearing it when she was here before."

She sat down beside her telephone.

"You had better hurry," she said.

10

THE front door to the downstairs apartment stood ajar, and from within came the murmur of quiet voices. Jerry frowned, walked inside. The living room looked barred after the cluttered decor of Mrs. Quarles' room. Stephanie was standing under the sunburst mirror.

"Oh, there you are, darling." She smiled warmly and turned to the two men with her — Finchley and de Ordas. "Jerry thought we had a burglar." She looked at Jerry. "Did you catch him, dear?"

"Yeah," he said shortly. "He's in my back pocket."

She saw the bandage on his head and gave an explanation of concern. "But you're hurt! What happened to you?"

"A door ran into me," he said.

127

Oliver Finchley sat primly on a maple chair near the casement windows. He didn't look drunk any more. De Ordas was at the spinet piano. He now wore a soft gray tweed and a knitted red tie and soft white shirt, but there was still a military air about him. He nodded blandly to Jerry.

"I hope I am not intruding. I beg a thousand pardons."

"One will be enough," said Jerry. He looked at the mirror over Stephanie's head, but the mirror spike was still missing. He wondered who had it, and whether it would be used again. He didn't like the thought, and turned back to de Ordas.

"How long have you been here?"

"Only five minutes. I came to talk to you, Señor Benedict."

Jerry said: "Does Castro's S.P.S. — *the Seguridad* — know you are here?"

The effect was extraordinary. The tall man stood up with a jolt, his eyes flicked back and forth, from Jerry to the girl, and he wet his lips before replying.

"*The Seguridad?*" he whispered.

"Castro's gunmen," Jerry said coldly. "I imagine they'd like to get their hands on you."

"You are joking?"

"Is it to be joked about?"

"I know nothing of it," de Ordas said. He sat down slowly, his eyes unwinking on Jerry. "Nothing at all."

Jerry turned to the girl. "I told you to let no one in."

"But I'm perfectly safe," she protested. "I have the gun." She took the little Colt from the mantel over the fireplace and held it up for all to see. "Besides, they insisted on waiting for you. They say they have a — a deal to propose."

Finchley spoke in precise tones, his tongue remarkably untangled now. "We decided to pool our resources, Benedict. We shall make it worth your while if you co-operate. We know what an inconvenience it will be to you and your charming wife, but it will be only a temporary — and profitable — arrangement."

Stephanie said helpfully: "They want this apartment for one week. After that, they'll turn it back to us."

"I'm afraid they're too late," Jerry said.

"Too late?" de Ordas asked politely.

"Gantredi's body has been found." He heard the girl's quick, surprised gasp, but he kept his eyes on the two men. They didn't pretend ignorance, but Finchley exhaled loudly and looked worried. Jerry went on: "Mrs. Quarles found the body in the coal bin when she went down to fix the fuses. She is calling the police." He paused. "I gather you both knew that Gantredi was dead."

Señor de Ordas nodded. "That is correct."

"Would it be too indiscreet to inquire which one of you killed him? And why?"

"We did not assassinate Mr. Gantredi," said de Ordas. "I happened to see you discover the body, that is all. That is how we knew about it. I told Mr. Finchley." He stood up. "However, I hardly relish the inquisitions of your admirable police department."

Stephanie said sharply: "Sit right down, *señor!*"

She held the gun pointed at all of them and moved across the room to stand beside Jerry, her shoulder brushing his arm. She wasn't as cool as she pretended. Her body was trembling.

Jerry turned back to the two men.

"I'm sure you have nothing to fear from the admirable police," he told de Ordas. "That is, if you didn't kill Mr. Gantredi, and if you both have adequate explanations."

Finchley chirruped: "But I was in the neighborhood all afternoon! I couldn't explain . . . "

De Ordas smiled with thin lips. "I, too, would not care to give any reason for my presence here."

"But you will," Jerry said. "To me,

or to the cops. Or would you prefer my going to your consulate with all this?"

The man's eyes were malignant. He half started for the door, then paused and shrugged military shoulders.

"As you wish," he said. "It is futile to run away now."

Jerry turned to the girl. "Were you with them both for the past fifteen minutes?" he asked.

Señor de Ordas said sharply: "She was not."

Steve looked distressed. "I — I stepped outside and followed you, Jerry. I wanted to see where you were going. But you had already disappeared, and I walked to the corner and stood there a few minutes — there'd been a fight in the corner taproom — and then I walked back. De Ordas and Finchley were already here when I returned."

"In the apartment?"

"No, in the lobby. I'd locked the door."

"Why didn't you stay here, as I asked you to?"

"I'm not a child," she said defensively. "Besides, I was worried about you."

She was too lovely for him to think straight about her. He watched morosely as she sat down on the couch, tucking shapely legs under her. De Ordas began to play the piano, very softly, an odd, sad little melody that was all sharps and flats. Jerry put on his hat.

"Where are you going now, Galahad?" she asked.

"The cops will be here any moment." He looked at her with dour interest. "Think you can take care of yourself?"

"If you're going out, what shall I tell the police?"

"I'll be right back," he said.

Shrugging, she turned to de Ordas at the piano. The Spaniard's dark hair glistened in the soft light.

"There's a Phil Baker-piano somewhere around," Stephanie said. "I'm sure I saw one before. If you'll wait, I'll accompany you. Can you play 'Coming Through the Rye?'"

Jerry felt angry. "It is a concertina and not an accordion, and it is in the study closet," he snapped. He felt belittled by the girl's calm competence. Whatever hesitation he had about leaving her alone disappeared. With her cool, mocking eyes, she was the sort of girl who would always control a situation through the men around her, and this irritated him, because he rather liked the idea of Stephanie being dependent on him alone.

He followed her into the little study. De Ordas and Finchley showed no signs of leaving. Shutting the door carefully, Jerry expelled a deep breath as the girl searched the closet for the concertina.

"I want to talk to you," he said. "Alone."

"I thought you were leaving us," she said. She came up with the big red concertina and faced him, impatient. "What is it?"

"Before the police come," he said, "I think you ought to know that Gantredi isn't our only problem."

"He isn't?"

He ignored her for a moment, crossing the room to examine the pink plastic telephone. The number on the dial was Waldorf — 9-6656. His mouth quirked with satisfaction as he returned to face the dark-haired girl.

"You've been feeling pretty secure up to now," he said. "You figured Hamilton would pull you out of this mess."

"And he will," said the girl.

Jerry said quietly: "No, he won't. He never will."

Her blue eyes grew slowly wider.

"I don't know what you mean — "

"Hamilton is dead," Jerry said bluntly. "He's upstairs, on the third floor. I just found him there. If you were counting on his help, you can forget it, here and now."

Before his gaze, he saw something crumple inside her, torn to ribbons by a gust of bitter anguish. A little whimpering sound came from her parted lips. He took a step toward her, but she straightened almost immediately, her face deathly pale.

"You're not lying?" she whispered.

"No."

"He was murdered?"

"Yes."

He wanted to take her in his arms as she sank slowly into a chair. Instead, he went to the door and looked toward the living room. De Ordas and Finchley were whispering together, urgently. When he looked back, the girl's eyes were firm and decisive again.

"I'll have to trust you," she said. "I'll need help."

"Now that Frank can't help you?"

She nodded. "I — I hardly knew him, really. But I felt that all those lies about his past — "

"They weren't lies," Jerry said.

"Maybe not. That explains why he told me never to reveal who I really am or what I meant to him. He said his enemies would try to reach him by threatening, or injuring me." The girl's long hands rested quietly in her lap. "I don't know what it was all about. Something to do with a lot of money, and Frank thought the others would believe I had it, if they knew who I am. I trusted Frank; I wanted to help him. I still do, even if he's dead. But now that I'm all alone . . ."

Jerry said: "You can trust me, Steve."

"I don't know," she said.

"What was Frank Hamilton to you?" he asked. "Will you tell me that much?"

She was silent, holding the red concertina in her lap. He waved his hand in a defeated gesture. "All right, you don't have to tell me anything you don't want to."

"It's just that — I'm terribly afraid now."

"I'll help you all I can, anyway," he said.

"What are we going to do now?" she asked. "Are the police really coming here?"

He nodded. "There's no use running away, either. They'd round us all up anyway, and it would look worse if you ran away."

"Very well," she said quietly. "Whatever you say, Jerry."

Some of the color had come back to her cheeks.

He hesitated, wanting to question her, aching to help her. But she stood up, self-reliant and calm again.

"We'd better make sure Finchley and de Ordas stay, too."

They went back to the living room, Stephanie carrying the concertina. The two men broke off their fierce whispering as they reappeared. De Ordas began to play the piano again. Jerry put the Colt down beside the girl.

"Keep your gun on these two," he said. "I'll be back soon."

"They won't get away," she said grimly.

★ ★ ★

The taxi was still parked on Harvey Street, outside of Ernie's Bar. The crowd outside the taproom was gone. The cabby woke up reluctantly.

"Regent Towers," Jerry said. "And quick."

"Oh, it's you again," said the cab driver. "You're giving me a neurosis."

Jerry leaned forward from the back seat and studied the hack driver's license. The man's face was broad and homely, with well-nourished cauliflower ears. His name was Joseph T. Schultz.

"A neurosis?" Jerry said, aggrieved. "What have I done?"

"You're always in a hurry," said Shultz. He clashed gears and tore around the first corner on two wheels. "Always rushin' around, like the world was on fire. Like my Uncle Jonathan. He's the one who married my Aunt Minnie. He finally wound up goin' off Brooklyn Bridge, doin' sixty. They took a long time to fish him out of the river, though, even after he spent his whole life rushin' around like you."

Jerry said: "Well, just take me to Regent Towers, Schultz. No bridges. You may lash the horses."

He settled back with a sigh, frowning at the rain as they rolled uptown. At West Seventieth, something clicked in his mind and he said:

"Do you know where a Dr. Polders' hospital is, around this neighborhood?"

Schultz guffawed.

"See? I told you so! I knew you'd wind up like that."

"Like what?" Jerry asked. "What's the matter now?"

"That's the place for rumdums," said the cab driver.

"Rumdums, hey?" Jerry felt pleased. "Let's postpone Regent Towers, Schultz. Let's go see the good doctor."

The private hospital was a four-story brick house hiding its age behind a modern façade. There were bars over the high, narrow windows, and an iron gate in a brick wall bordering the sidewalk. The gate wasn't locked. A card in the doors said, *Ring and*

140

Walk In. Jerry tried the door, found it open, and walked in without ringing.

There was a bleached mahogany table, an umbrella stand, and gaily colored murals on the vestibule wall which didn't make much sense when Jerry paused to interpret them. An antiseptic smell cloyed the air. Someone was giggling softly from behind a nearby door, a steady ripple of falsetto sound that went on and on without any apparent pause for breath. Jerry didn't investigate. He started down the hall and a man stepped quietly from somewhere to his right and halted beside him — a very big young man with thick black hair, football shoulders, and a chin that was a terrible disappointment to the rest of his physique.

"I'm Albert," said the young man gently. His brows made a thick, heavy ridge over his small eyes. "May I help you?"

"I want to see Dr. Polders," Jerry said.

"Yes sir. What did you want to see him about?"

"Mrs. Quarles sent me," said Jerry. "I believe she works here."

A woman began screaming somewhere on an upper floor. The sound spiraled upward in wild ululations, then was abruptly cut off by the loud slam of a door. Albert paid no attention.

"And what is your name, sir?"

"Twist," said Jerry. "Oliver Q. Twist."

Albert murmured: "If you will wait here . . . "

He moved rapidly down the hall to a door at the far end. Jerry waited until he had disappeared, then followed. The door wasn't locked. In modern, raised silver lettering the name *james j polders* appeared on the walnut panel. Jerry stepped through the doorway into an office that was a symphony in green — presumably restful to the patients. The walls were the color of fresh spring grass, and the leather chairs were a pale lemonish hue. A green marble miniature of Bernini's baroque statue

142

of David was the only ornament on the desk. The floor was a checkerboard of contrasting shades of emerald.

Albert was talking to the man who sat behind the desk.

"I don't know who he is, but he mentioned Lucy Quarles, so I didn't throw him out." He turned, saw Jerry in the doorway, and said, less gently: "I thought I told you to wait in the hall."

Jerry ignored him. The man at the desk, in a starched white medical coat, had familiar red hair, freckles, and watery green eyes. He looked a great deal like Mr. Holovacs, the shy bridegroom from High Corners, Kansas. In fact, he was Mr. Holovacs.

Jerry grinned. "Mr. Holovacs, I presume?"

Albert said: "This is Dr. Polders."

"Errors will happen," said Jerry pleasantly. He still grinned at the man behind the desk. Dr. Polders frowned and flushed with anger. Staring at Jerry, he jerked a thumb toward the door and said: "Albert. Leave us."

"But he — " Albert began.

"Go!"

Albert vanished.

Dr. Polders leaned back in his chair, and looked at Jerry with unfriendly eyes.

"You're Benedict, the man who got that apartment. How did you find me here? Did Lucy Quarles tell you who I was? I was sure she hadn't seen me."

"It was pure happen-chance," Jerry said. "Don't blame Mrs. Quarles. I just came for a little information."

"I have none to give you."

Jerry moved a chair against the wall with his toe and sat down in it without removing his hands from his raincoat pockets. He hoped Dr. Polders would think he had a gun hidden there.

"You can talk to me, or talk to the cops," Jerry said. "You have a choice, admittedly. But I assure you, it will be better to talk to me first."

"Is that a threat?" Polders looked amused. "I can have you thrown out of here in five seconds flat."

Jerry nodded. "Albert has cute hands. I'll bet he gets quite a kick out of bouncing your patients off the walls."

"Albert has his doctorate in psychiatry." Polders played with his bony hands, put them on his knees, looked at Jerry's coat pockets, and licked his lips. "Just what would you like to know?"

"I came here, originally, just to check up on Mrs. Quarles' statement that she was employed here, but I see that it isn't necessary. Now that I've learned you are Dr. Polders, I can see a lot of other possibilities. I want to know how it came about that Mrs. Quarles sent Frank Hamilton here, and when, and why; and how long you kept Hamilton in this private belfry and when you released him."

Dr. Polders' freckles stood out against the ashen pallor of his face. "And who is Hamilton?"

"You know," Jerry sighed, "but I'll tell you. He's the man whose apartment you were so anxious to rent this evening. By the way, who are the Holovacs, anyway?"

"Cousins of mine." Dr. Polders fished for a cigarette in his white jacket pocket, decapitated Bernini's David with a flick of his thumb, and revealed a lighter in the statuette. It seemed sacrilegious to Jerry. Leaning back, the doctor said: "You've made some rather startling statements about my patients. It seems to me that it's a question of professional ethics."

"It certainly is," said Jerry.

Dr. Polders looked ethical.

"Then I don't see how I can tell you anything."

Jerry said sharply: "The cops might be interested in knowing why you tried to rent that apartment after Hamilton had been a patient here."

"Why should the police enter this?"

"They're habitually curious about homicide," Jerry said.

"Homicide?" Dr. Polders' mouth twitched angrily. "Hamilton may not have been in perfect health when he left my care, but he certainly wasn't dead! I — "

Jerry said quietly:

"Then he *was* a patient of yours?"

Polders looked at him with annoyed, watery eyes.

"I don't know how you learned this, or whether you merely guessed, but I have nothing to hide, you see. My cards are all on the table. Hamilton came here two weeks ago with a very severe cranial concussion inflicted by the proverbial blunt instrument. He said he had been in an accident, and gave his name as Gerald Reese, and he paid for treatment in advance, with cash. He had quite a lot of cash on his person. I did not, however, expect him to live."

"But he walked in here by himself?"

"Yes. He was shocked, dazed — in a state of collapse."

"Did you report it to the police?"

"You know I did not."

"Why not?"

Polders shrugged. "He was well-dressed, apparently of a good background, and he wouldn't have chosen my establishment unless he wanted to avoid publicity. In addition, let us say that I did not know his true identity at the time. He was simply a Mr. Gerald Reese. I did not connect him with the disappearance of Frank Hamilton. In any case, I have nothing to fear from the police."

"That's what you think," Jerry said. "Did he have any visitors? Did he notify anybody at all that he was alive?"

"A woman named Wanda Dykes came to see him once," Polders nodded. "That was on the fourth day after he was admitted here. He sent for her himself and she visited him daily after that. She was the only one, though."

"How did you learn that Reese was Frank Hamilton?"

"Mrs. Quarles knew yesterday, and Albert happened to overhear their conversation."

"Then Mrs. Quarles knew yesterday that your patient was Hamilton, and that he wasn't dead, as reported in the papers?"

"That is true."

"And Hamilton was here all this time, until yesterday?"

"Until this morning. That's when he disappeared."

"Disappeared?"

"He was found missing at ten o'clock this morning. He ran away, you see. He had no business being up and out of bed. If he is dead now, as you imply, I am not in the least surprised. The shock of his wound, and whatever exertions he went through to effect his escape — his unauthorized release — would most certainly cause a severe relapse, if not death."

Jerry said: "But he didn't die of shock or a cracked skull. He was murdered, doctor, at Number 16 Waverly Walk — just a short while ago."

Dr. Polders quivered. Jerry made no effort to stop him as he pressed a button on the desk, but kept to his seat, with his back to the wall.

Dr. Polders cleared his throat.

"Murdered, you say?"

"Murdered," Jerry repeated.

"That's quite interesting. Are the police there now?"

"By now, yes," said Jerry.

"Do they know about me?"

"Not yet."

The doctor seemed relieved. He looked up as Albert entered in answer to his summons. The big young man leaned his meaty shoulders against the wall. His face was utterly blank.

"Yes, doctor?"

Dr. Polders nodded at Jerry.

"Mr. Benedict will be staying with us for a while."

Jerry said: "Oh, no, I'm not."

Polders said: "I don't think he has a gun, Albert. He's bluffing."

"Yes, sir," said Albert. He turned, licked his lips, and crossed the office toward Jerry. "Be nice, Mr. Benedict. You'll be quite comfortable here. We're all one big happy family — "

Jerry put his hands on the arm of his chair, braced himself, and kicked the big man in the knee. Albert howled. Dr. Polders yanked at a desk drawer and clawed frantically inside. Jerry came out of his chair with a swift, smooth rush, snatched up the marble statuette of David, and slammed it down on Polders' hand. A small gun skittered across the shining desk and thudded to the checkerboard floor. Polders made a sound like a horse whinnying and staggered back against the window blinds, wringing his smashed fingers.

Something hard and heavy landed on Jerry's back, sent him staggering as Albert's long arms whipped around his neck in a deadly judo grip. Jerry squirmed, reached for a hold on the big man. His larynx was being crushed, and he realized with a sudden rush of panic that he was in mortal danger. His lungs screamed for air. Bending his knees he closed desperate fingers on Albert's shoulders and flipped the big man over his head. The strangle hold was abruptly broken. Albert flew through the air and slammed against the far wall with a thud.

Jerry straightened, took a deep, burning breath, and saw Dr. Polders reaching for the gun on the floor. He brought his heel down heavily on the doctor's hand. Polders screamed and gave up all efforts at the gun. Jerry scooped it up and covered his two opponents. He was shaking with rage.

"Now behave," he gasped.

The gun was an Italian Beretta, a .38, and felt snug in his grip. His fingers trembled and felt weak. Polders was out cold on the green floor, and his hand didn't look much like a hand any more. Albert was sitting up with his back against the opposite wall, his face moronic.

There came a quick rap on the door, and Joe Schultz, the cab driver, peered in, looked around, and saw Jerry with the gun in his hand. A surprised expression crossed his big face. He pocketed the blackjack he was carrying.

"Hi, chum," he said. "Are you all right? You're running up an awful bill on my meter."

"I'm fine," said Jerry. He put the Beretta in his pocket. "Let's get the hell out of here."

Schultz was looking with clinical interest at Dr. Polders, sprawled on the floor.

"What's the matter with him?"

"He's suffering from an acute neurosis," Jerry said.

11

THE rain came down in wide, blustery curtains, drumming on the marquee of the Regent Towers Hotel. A black-faced clock on the wall read 10:22. The clerk's desk in the lobby was a symphony of glass in black and silver. Poinsettias stood in deep vases at the base of the square-cut piers that supported the ceiling.

Jerry ignored the clerk's arched eyebrows and crossed at a casual saunter to the elevators. The operator was a straw-haired boy with an alert face and superior eyes.

"Miss Dykes' apartment, please," Jerry said.

"Is she expecting you, sir?" asked the boy. It was that kind of an apartment house, one where the tenants were wrapped in guarded seclusion from all common irritants of the day. Jerry took a five-dollar bill from his wallet, added another five to it, folded them lengthwise in his fingers. He said again: "Miss Dykes' apartment."

The boy took the two bills.

"Yes, sir."

At the seventeenth floor, the boy let the doors slide open with a soft, refined hiss of air, and said: "You a cop, mister?"

"Would a cop give away ten bucks?" Jerry asked.

"No. I guess I'm dumb," said the boy. He said it with no conviction at all. "You aren't going to make any trouble up here, are you?"

"Is it the custom?" Jerry asked.

"Well, she has some pretty nifty friends. That George Chalett, for example — he scares hell out of me every time he comes in."

"He scares hell out of me, too. Does he visit often?"

"Only lately."

"How lately?"

"The last couple of weeks." The

elevator door started to close at last. "Well, be good. It's 17-D you want, buddy."

Jerry waited until the elevator was on its way down, then walked slowly along a hushed, perfumed corridor to Wanda Dykes' suite and thumbed the ivory button to produce the sound of muted chimes. He took off his hat and smoothed his unruly red hair and waited until high heels clicked and a maid opened the door for him. She stared at him.

His weariness vanished abruptly. The maid had rich auburn hair, a cupid's-bow mouth, and a tight, smooth black dress designed to accentuate a somewhat plump figure. Her lipstick was awry and her hair was slightly disheveled. She looked at Jerry with pale eyes that widened slowly to the size of poker chips.

Jerry said happily:

"Fancy meeting you here, Mrs. Holovacs!"

The girl gasped and tried to slam the

door in his face. Jerry stopped it with his foot and shoved hard. The maid fell back three steps, her bosom rising and falling with her quick breathing.

"You're making a mistake," she said. She kept her voice low. "I'll call the manager."

"It's no mistake," he said.

She tried another tack. "Please," she whispered. "Don't tell Miss Dykes."

From within the apartment, a woman's voice called: "Who is it, Apple?"

The maid stared fearfully at Jerry. He smiled and handed her his hat. She took it mechanically. He decided that she looked rather attractive in the tight black dress.

"I've just come from Dr. Polders," he said. He studied her smeared lipstick. "You both make a fine couple, Apple."

"Oh, we're not married," Apple said quickly. "I can explain it all, if you'll just give me a chance." Her hands fluttered and she dropped his hat, stooped, and picked it up again. "It

157

was all John's idea — Dr. Polders', I mean — to rent that place. He used to know Hamilton, 'way back."

Jerry was pleased. "He knew Hamilton in the old days?"

"He used to work for him. But please don't give me away to Miss Dykes. She doesn't even know we were there. That's why we — Dr. Polders and I — had to slip away when she showed up."

"Just how far away did you slip?"

"Why, I came here. John went back to his office."

"*Apple!*" It was Wanda Dykes' voice, crackling with impatience. "Who is it?"

"It's Mr. Benedict," the maid called back.

There was a moment's spinning silence. Then:

"Tell him I won't see him!"

Jerry took the silk scarf he had found on the third floor at Waverly Walk, and rippled it through his fingers. Apple's eyes widened. "Tell her I found this at Number 16."

Apple relayed the information. There was more silence. Then Wanda's rich voice came again from the back of the apartment. It sounded as if there were several doors in between.

"Have him wait. And come in here, Apple."

The maid appealed to Jerry again with her eyes. He said softly: "It's all right. But I'll want to talk to you later."

He followed her into a long room decorated in old ivory and pale blue. There was a wide leopard-skin couch with bleached mahogany arms near the marble fireplace and maroon drapes over tall windows that apparently opened onto a terrace. The power-blue carpet had an abstract design in white going jaggedly from one corner to the other. Jerry began to follow the white path by placing one foot, heel to toe, directly ahead of the other. The path ended in a small bar standing open against the wall. He tried the decanter. It was excellent Canadian rye. He kept his arms outstretched as if he were walking a tightrope and watched a cigarette smoulder in a turquoise ash tray. There was no lipstick on the cigarette end.

Apple came in and stared at his acrobatic pose and said: "Please wait in here. Miss Dykes is taking a shower."

Jerry nodded and didn't drop his precarious position until she disappeared through french doors. Then he inquisitively opened the nearest closet door. Wanda's gray satin raincoat hung there, dripping on the parquetry floor.

The french doors opened into a hall where his hat rested on a small gateleg table. He picked it up as Apple came along carrying a folded blue turkish bath towel. Before she could protest, he followed her through the bathroom door.

"Miss Dykes will have to dress!" she exclaimed.

"But I'm in a hurry," Jerry said.

The bathroom was almost as large as the living room, all black and gold and paneled with blue-tinted mirrors. The scent of magnolias was overpowering. From behind a frosted shower door decorated with red flamingos came Wanda's amused laughter.

"If that's Mr. Benedict, it's all right, Apple. Get my housecoat."

The maid measured Jerry's six feet with speculative eyes, and walked out. After a moment Wanda stepped from the shower closet, her hair done up in a tight golden knot on top of her fine Grecian head. Her tanned shoulders were bare. Her eyes laughed as she held the big blue bath towel in front of her. She held it at her throat, and he could see the outline of her body on either side. She wore only the towel — and her lipstick.

"You wanted to see me?" she asked.

"Not quite so much of you," Jerry said. He resisted the temptation to look over her shoulder. "You're forgetting the mirrors, Miss Dykes."

The blonde smiled.

"Am I?"

He felt very warm suddenly. Apple came in with the housecoat and stood between them as the blonde stepped into it. The housecoat was a long-sleeved affair with a zipper to the throat. Gold sequins were sprayed across the shoulders. The tall girl stepped into gold slippers and said:

"We'll be more comfortable in the living room, Mr. Benedict."

He got crème de cocoa for her and a rye highball for himself, lit two cigarettes, and sank down beside her on the long leopard-skin couch. Now that he had an opportunity for close inspection, he could see why Wanda Dykes was the toast of the nightclub circuit. Her blondeness was genuine, he knew that; and her eyes were a pale, lucidly amused jade. But her mouth, rich and full, gave evidence at the corners of what might be a violent temper.

"Apple said you came to return my scarf," she remarked. "How sweet of you."

Jerry took the band of silk from his pocket and dropped it on the coffee table. The girl didn't touch it. She picked a fleck of tobacco from her red underlip and watched him guardedly.

"I was wondering where I had lost it," she said.

"I found it at No. 16 Waverly Walk," Jerry said. He added casually: "It was lying beside a dead man."

Her face gave away nothing at all. She said:

"Oh, you mean Gantredi."

He didn't correct her.

She went on: "It's a clumsy attempt to frame me, of course."

"Of course," said Jerry.

"You're so sweet. I like you. I like redheaded men." She got up, her long coat swishing, and put out her cigarette in the turquoise ash tray.

When she sat down, she was considerably closer to Jerry. He looked at the tall terrace windows, but resisted an impulse to change his position. The blonde girl said: "You're after some

163

information, of course. But why do you think I'll tell you what you want to know, even if I know it?"

"Because you're in a spot," Jerry said. "You see, I've just had an interesting chat with a fellow who calls himself Dr. Polders. He spells his name with little letters, and runs a clinic for hopheads, uptown. You know the place."

She called Polders a very unflattering name.

"Did he tell you I'd been there?"

"He said you'd been to see Frank Hamilton," Jerry nodded.

"That does put me in a spot, doesn't it? It's rather awkward. What do you want to know?"

He felt a wave of admiration for her.

"You save me a lot of coercion," he said.

"I'm just being sensible," the girl said. "But I really can't help you very much. I don't know who killed that Gantredi fellow."

"How did you know he had been killed?"

"I heard Señor de Ordas tell Finchley that you had found the body. That's why we all decided to clear out of there."

"What were you all looking for in that apartment?"

She laughed softly. "As if you didn't know!"

"As if I didn't," Jerry agreed. "Tell me."

"You're the expert on drawing pictures, but — well, we're trying to locate Pedro's money."

"Pedro?"

"Pedro de Ordas. That South American."

"What money is that?"

The girl sipped her tiny glass of crème de cocoa and regarded the fireplace. The logs weren't lighted. Rain beat lazily on the terrace flagstones beyond the tall windows.

"It was gambling syndicate money," she said. "Maybe half a million. Frank Hamilton had a lot of those big bills which he couldn't spend or deposit because of the Treasury crack-down on big bills. Frank had planned to exchange that currency with Señor de Ordas, as a sort of foreign outlet."

"What did de Ordas intend to do with this hot money?"

"Take it back to Argentina. There's a market there for U.S. currency in large denominations. Officially, Pedro is here on some financial mission, and I suppose he saw this way to make a private coup for himself."

"I guess that's why he's so concerned about the police putting him in the limelight," Jerry suggested wryly. "I'd be concerned, too, if I thought the Cuban S.P.S. was hunting me for swiping revolutionary funds."

He betrayed no excitement at the girl's revelation. It was warm in the apartment. He wished she wouldn't sit quite so close to him: on the other hand, he had no regrets. He asked: "Who else knew about this money? Finchley? And George Chalett?"

Wanda nodded. "The whole deal was

arranged right here in this apartment. Both of them turned in their big bills to Hamilton, to be exchanged — at a discount, of course — for Pedro's smaller ones. Hamilton really acted only as middleman. The thing is, he disappeared *after* he had collected the hot bills from Finchley and George Chalett, but *before* he made the swap with Pedro for the smaller ones. So he had both sides' money when he vanished. And we can't find any of it. When I saw the ad, I thought it would be a good chance to move in and search at my leisure. But the others all had the same idea. George was awfully angry when he saw me there. He thought I was doublecrossing him, too." She looked at him. "But you know all this, anyway, or you wouldn't have been there yourself."

Jerry said: "Just one thing. You knew Frank was alive at Polders' hospital. Did the others know that?"

She frowned. "No, I didn't tell anybody."

"Then weren't you taking a chance, knowing Frank was still alive? He's not the sort of guy you doublecross lightly."

"Dr. Polders said I needn't expect Frank to live. He was too seriously injured."

Jerry scowled, chewed his thumbnail.

"Who's been visiting Frank's apartment for the last few days? Was it you?"

Her long jade eyes conceded admiration. "You know about that, too, I see. That Apple! I told her time and again to be sure to clean up the place after us. I took her with me several times while I searched the place, and we often stayed overnight and she cooked a little. Apple knows what this is all about, too. I trust her implicitly."

Jerry thought of the maid's smeared lipstick, but he didn't say anything about it.

"Then it was you who slashed all the furniture in the apartment?" he asked.

"Oh, no, that was done before."

"By whom?"

"I don't know. One of the others, I suppose."

"Who slugged Frank?" he asked. "And how did he get into Doc Polders' rabbit hutch?"

"I don't know. Maybe he got there himself. He knew Polders. He came out of his coma only once, to give Polders my name and ask for me. He never could speak to me on any of my visits." She leaned a little closer to Jerry. "Frank never told me anything at all, so I thought it best to rent the apartment outright when Polders told me that Frank didn't have much chance of living out the day."

Jerry said: "But I saw Frank less than an hour ago."

He had reached her this time. She lifted one hand in dismay, and stared at him with wide, frightened eyes.

"But where?" she asked in a whisper. "At Polders' place?"

"No. At Waverley Walk."

"You're lying," she said tightly.

"No, I'm not."

"But was he all right?"

"That depends on your point of view," Jerry said.

The color drained from her face.

"Then he's dead," she whispered. "That's what you mean. He must have recovered consciousness and tried to get back home. It's unbelievable. And then he collapsed, I suppose."

Jerry said: "You might call it a collapse. Anybody would collapse with a knife in his back."

The half smile on Wanda's lips was slowly erased. Her body went stiff, and she spoke in a barely audible whisper.

"A knife?"

"He was murdered, angel. And that's where I found your scarf. Not beside Gantredi, but with Frank Hamilton."

Shock was followed by disbelief and then a wild, furious fear flamed in her pale eyes. Her hands fluttered out, touching him, imploring him. She leaned very close, and he could feel the warmth of her body through the housecoat.

"It can't be true," she whispered. "You're trying to frighten me. He wasn't murdered!"

A sudden loudening of the rain came from the terrace windows, along with a quick gust of chill, moist wind. Jerry tried to sit up, suddenly alarmed, but the girl's arms pinned him back in the deep couch for a moment. Her lips covered his mouth, hard and lingeringly, as she pressed against him.

Then a man's cool voice spoke from behind him.

"All right, ducky. Let him up for air."

Jerry flung the girl aside, feeling her long nails rake venomously across his cheek. Her housecoat ripped with a soft shredding sound as he tore away and lunged swiftly to his feet, reaching for the little Beretta in his pocket.

The gun was gone.

The girl was standing by the fireplace, calmly trying to assemble the pieces of her tattered robe.

"I've got it, stupid," she said.

She held the gun pointed at him, her face calm and amused again. Jerry turned to the man who had come in from the terrace, and his rage mounted. It was George Chalett. The gambler was still dressed in his neat derby and immaculate chesterfield. There was a Luger in his gray-gloved left hand, also pointed at Jerry. Behind the gambler stood Apple, the maid. She had changed from her tight black uniform to a green street dress, and wore a green felt hat to go with it. She looked frightened.

Chalett turned to the blonde.

"You didn't have to tell him as much as you did, ducky. You made it tough for him. Now he knows too much." He held out his hand. "Give me his gun."

Wanda Dykes shook her head.

"I'll keep it," she said. "Just get Stupid out of here, George. I don't care what you do with him. And don't come back yourself, either." Her voice tightened. "Don't ever come back to see me again."

Chalett lifted polite eyebrows.

"Something bothering you?"

"Frankie is bothering me," said Wanda. Frank bothers me a lot."

"If Benedict is telling the truth," said Chalett.

"He's telling the truth," Wanda said tightly. "You know he is. You ought to know."

Comprehension dawned in the gambler's neat, square face. He touched his waxed moustache with a fingertip.

"You think *I* killed Frank, ducky?"

"I don't know. Just get out of here, and leave me alone."

Chalett said: "Give me Stupid's gun, then."

Jerry said: "Do you trust him implicitly, too? Like you trust Apple?"

Apple said swiftly: "Shut up, you! Shut up!"

Wanda was startled. Apple, too, seemed surprised at the sound of her own voice. She looked guiltily at the gambler.

"It seems to me," Jerry said, "You're all trying to cross each other. Wanda tries to cross you, George, by going to that apartment alone, to see what she could pick up; and Apple was there, too, did you know that? She rang in Dr. Polders and the two of them tried to get into the place." Jerry grinned at Chalett. "And you ought to wipe off the gal's lipstick, George. It's a different shade from Wanda's."

Wanda's voice cracked sharply. "You mean Apple and George — while I was dressing — ?" Her jade eyes darkened with new fury. Violence edged into her words, directed at her secretary-maid. "Why, you cheap chisler, I'll — "

Her attention was fully diverted to the other couple. Jerry's lank figure uncoiled explosively from the couch driving toward the blonde. She gasped, whirled, tried to bring her gun up. His fingers closed around her wrist and twisted hard. The girl gasped again, her body slamming against him. There came another ripping sound from her housecoat as Jerry yanked her around to cover himself.

Wanda whimpered: "Don't shoot, George."

The gambler was very still. The corners of his mouth grew tight as Jerry closed his fingers on the girl's gun, flipped it around, and pointed it at him.

"Just stay like that, duckies," Jerry rapped.

Chalett's Luger came up. He was going to shoot. Jerry felt Wanda shudder. her body was alive with fear. Without warning, he shoved her hard toward the gambler. Chalett's gun blasted thunderously. The bullet smashed into the wall, and the next moment Wanda crashed into him. Jerry swung hard around the couch, his gun up, covering Chalett as the gambler staggered off balance. The Luger was pointed at the floor.

"Drop your gun, George," Jerry said.

Wanda backed away, futilely draping the shredded robe about her figure. Chalett's face turned impassive, except for a disgusted glance at Wanda. Then he shrugged and slid his weapon to the coffee table. The air was acrid with the smell of gunsmoke.

"Stupid is as stupid does," said Jerry.

He felt a little awed at having thrown a gun on George Chalett. The gambler's eyes mirrored fleeting shadows of future vengeance as they met Jerry's.

Jerry said: "Now we'll all go back to Waverly Walk and talk it over."

Wanda said: "I'll have to get dressed first." She was practically nude. She added in a flat, defeated tone: "It will take me a little time."

"Five minutes," said Jerry. "Then you go as you are. If you skip out of the back door, I'll send the cops after you."

The doorbell suddenly chimed.

The notes vibrated in the still, hushed

air, then were followed by a tremendous knocking. Nobody stirred. The bell chimed again, and a voice thundered:

"Open up in there!"

Jerry waggled his gun at Apple.

"Let them in, baby."

The maid hesitated, then vanished into the little foyer. Chalett said scornfully:

"That sounds like the cops. You don't want the cops here."

It occurred to Jerry that there was some truth in what the gambler said. It would have been fine if he voluntarily brought in the trio by himself; it might have squared things with Dulcey. But to be picked up like this, as if he were just another prisoner among them, added to all his other misdemeanors of the evening, would definitely not look good. But he had no time to give this more than fleeting consideration before Apple came sullenly into the room.

"Detectives Bakerman and Pease," she announced. "Of the Homicide Squad."

The two men entered the room hard on Apple's heels. Bakerman still looked big and clumsy. There was a new ketchup stain on his cardigan sweater, and he kept his coat swinging loosely open. Pease looked like a little weasel beside him, his sharp eyes in their smudged sockets jerking around erratically. His voice was shrill as he yanked out a gun that looked like a howitzer.

"We got 'em, Harvey. We got 'em all." He looked at Jerry and screamed: "Drop that gun, you rat!"

Jerry winced and hastily let go of the Beretta. Bakerman drawled: "Slow down, Peasey," and strolled around the leopard-skin couch, and said to Jerry: "You're in trouble screwball. The lieutenant wants to see you. You were supposed to stay out of this goddam case. And I wish you had, Jerry."

Jerry said: "What about all these others? Aren't you going to take Chalett in, too?"

Pease screamed: "Shut up, you rat!"

"We'll take you all in," Bakerman decided. His manner was easy, unexcited. "We don't have instructions on anybody but you, Jerry, but I guess we'll take you all in, all right."

Chalett said: "Officer, you're making a mistake. This man created a disturbance and finished by attacking Miss Dykes. I fired to protect her. The others will testify to that."

Bakerman grinned. "You can take it up with your lawyer."

"What does Dulcey want me for, exactly?" Jerry asked.

Bakerman helped himself to a cigarette from the coffee table. The creases around his mouth deepened as he lit it.

"Murder," he said casually.

"Me?" Jerry asked, aggrieved.

"Could be. Did you really attack Miss Dykes?"

Pease snarled impatiently: "Ah, let's get going, Harve!"

Wanda Dykes made an imperious sniffing sound and said haughtily:

"Well, I can't go like this! You'll have to let me get dressed."

The attention of the two detectives centered on the blonde and her state of déshabille. Pease's mouth grew slack with a lewd grin. Bakerman lost some of his bored, weary expression.

"Don't let us rush you, sister," said Pease.

"To hell with you," said Wanda. "You're drooling."

She let go of the shredded housecoat and stepped completely out of it without losing an inch of dignity. She stood as regally as a queen while the silk rustled to the carpet at her feet, and then she walked, completely nude, out of the room.

Pease just stared, open-mouthed.

Bakerman sighed and smoothed his gray hair.

"A policeman's lot," he said, "ain't always an unhappy one."

12

TWO squad cars were parked on the rainy cobblestones of Waverly Walk, their white hoods glistening under the antique street lamp. A knot of morbid onlookers jostled each other with umbrellas and eyed the belligerent young cop who blocked the doorway to Number 16. Two more cops were in the lobby, with a white-coated attendant from the medical examiner's office, and three reporters. Kennedy, from the *Times*, said: "Hello, master mind. You should have stuck to the funny papers." He rolled his eyes dramatically to the ceiling. "And the murderer was brought back to the scene of his crime!"

Bakerman nudged Jerry into the apartment. The big living room was crowded with fingerprint men, police photographers, and more plainclothes

181

detectives. Señor de Ordas directed dark, venomous eyes at Jerry as he entered. Oliver Finchley perched on the very edge of his chair. Wanda Dykes took a chair for herself, apart from Chalett and Apple. The lethal spoke from the sunburst mirror was still missing.

Stephanie Farley was nowhere in sight.

"Where's the lieutenant?" Bakerman asked.

"Still in the cellar," someone nodded. "Just waiting."

Bakerman guided Jerry down the rickety wooden staircase. The cellar, flooded with light, reached cavernously back to the rear of the house. The entire contents of the coal bin had been piled ruthlessly against the white plaster walls, and the coal bin itself stood empty except for Lieutenant Dulcey. The lieutenant's sallow cheeks were smeared with coal dust. Steve wasn't down here, either. Dulcey adjusted the owlish pince-nez that made him look ten years older than his confessed forty and glared at Jerry.

"So, Benedict. Let's go upstairs," he said.

"Is this where you found Gantredi?" Jerry asked.

"You ought to know."

They trooped up into the small study. Apparently Dulcey had made this room his command post. The rain no longer beat against the barred windows. Resting mountainously on the red leather couch was Lucius McConaughy. He looked like an enormous Buddha, and he stared at Jerry with misgivings. Jerry felt misgivings, too. For the first time, he wondered just how serious the charges were against him. It would have to be something pretty tight to bring McConaughy down to bat for him.

Dulcey said to the fat man: "You are not to interrupt, Mr. McConaughy. You may stay only on condition that I ask the questions." He looked at Jerry with hostile eyes, dabbed at his blackened cheek with a handkerchief and waved to a chair. "Sit down, Benedict."

Jerry selected a spindly wooden chair. "Where's the girl?" he asked.

"I'll ask the questions," Dulcey repeated. His lips were thin, uncompromising. "Forget about the girl."

Jerry was alarmed. "Where is she? What kind of cops are you, anyway?"

McConaughy rumbled: "Take it easy, Jerry. I warned you to get off this story. Now Cy wants to book you for murder."

"Which one?" Jerry asked.

Dulcey said: "Oh, is there more than one?"

Jerry blinked. "What did the girl tell you?"

"I haven't talked to any girl. Nobody knows anything about a girl. Who is she?"

"Stephanie Farley," Jerry said. "She was here when I left."

Waving his hand, Dulcey said: "Well, we'll discuss her later. There are a few questions . . . "

"We'll discuss her now," Jerry said angrily. "I want her located. She had my gun, which I gave to her, and I want to know what happened to her after I left."

"Evidently she skipped out," Dulcey suggested.

"She didn't skip. Something must have happened to her." Jerry paused, his anxiety growing. He looked around the little study. "Wait a minute. Where is the concertina?"

Pease stood at the doorway and sneezed.

"This guy is nuts, Lieutenant. First he talks about a girl nobody's seen, then a concertina."

"Well, they're both missing!" Jerry insisted. "And they were both here before!"

Dulcey said quietly: "Relax, Benedict. We want your cooperation, that's all. We want to know everything you know about this crime. Help us, and we'll help you. After all, we've worked pretty well together, before this." He spread his hands and sat back in his chair like a college professor. "You implied there was more than one murder committed here, didn't you? What was that all about?"

"Did I?" Jerry asked. He looked stubborn.

"You distinctly said, 'Which one?' when I asked you." Dulcey leaned forward over the desk. "All we've got is Gantredi. He was in the coal bin, but there wasn't much blood around, so we know he wasn't killed there. Is that where you last saw him, by the way?"

"No."

"Where, then?"

"In the closet, here in this room."

"You were the last one to see Gantredi, weren't you?"

"Me?" Jerry asked blankly.

"You rented this apartment from him, didn't you?"

"No, I never saw him at all — not while he was living, anyway."

Dulcey pawed at the papers on the

desk, picked up a scrap from among the litter, and held it up plainly for all to see.

"What about this rent receipt, then? Gantredi's signature is on it, and it's made out to you. How can you deny having seen him?" he asked triumphantly.

"I forged it," Jerry said.

McConaughy groaned, ran pudgy fingers through his curly hair, and bowed his head. Dulcey nodded, pleased.

"So you forged it," he repeated heavily.

"I had to," Jerry explained. "Everybody was waiting around for Gantredi, and only Steve and I knew that he was already dead, so I faked the rent receipt in order to be sure I'd get the lease on this apartment."

"How did you know Gantredi was already dead?"

"I told you, Steve and I found him here in the closet."

"But Mrs. Quarles found the body in the cellar."

"Well, somebody moved him," Jerry shrugged.

"What for?"

"How should I know?"

"Who moved him?"

"I don't know," Jerry said. "Maybe you ought to ask Steve."

"Did Steve move him?"

"I've told you — Steve is that girl, and she's missing."

Dulcey said: "I know all about that girl. Are your sure you feel quite well, Benedict?"

Jerry slumped back in his chair. "I feel awful, he said. "I think I'm going to chew up the carpet."

Dulcey exchanged a significant glance with McConaughy and sighed. "Look here, Jerry, we know you've been working hard on the *Globe*, you've overworked, really. McConaughy asked me to make allowances for that." Jerry looked in mild amazement at the fat man on the couch. Dulcey went on: "I'm perfectly willing to accept the idea that you've acted with the best of intentions. I'm even willing to assume that a certain sum of money we believe hidden here — we know more than you credit us with, you see — I'm willing to assume that the money did not prove too great a temptation for you."

"So now I'm a crook," Jerry said indignantly.

"Not at all. But you're giving us a picture as cockeyed as your cartoons. We know there was a lot of money here."

Jerry said suddenly: "I think I know where it is. I think I know where Frank Hamilton hid it. He put it away so that nobody — not even you, when you were here before — could find it."

Dulcey smiled and leaned forward eagerly.

"Now we're getting somewhere. Where is the money, Jerry?"

"In the concertina," Jerry said.

Dulcey grew apoplectic. "*What* concertina?" he bellowed.

"The one Steve had when I left. It's not around now, and neither is Steve.

Or did I mention that before?"

"All right." Dulcey relaxed with a sigh, and spoke as if to a stubborn child. "Just who was here when you skipped out?"

"Señor de Ordas and Finchley," Jerry said. "And I didn't skip, I walked out, and I left the girl with them."

Dulcey turned to Pease, who promptly sneezed.

"Get 'em," he directed.

The tall Argentine nodded gravely to one and all as he entered. Finchley trailed him timidly. Both men regarded McConaughy's great bulk with some astonishment and waited while the lieutenant tried to stare them down.

"This man," said Dulcey, indicating Jerry, "insists he left you in this house in the presence of a girl named Stephanie Farley. All I want is a simple answer. Was such a girl here tonight?"

Señor de Ordas shook his head. "There was no girl."

Finchley echoed him. "No, no girl."

"Of all the conniving — " Jerry

started up from his chair, pale with anger. Bakerman shoved him down in the seat again. Dulcey spread his hands with a pleased smile.

"See? No girl."

"Well, ask Mrs. Quarles, then!" Jerry stormed. "She knows about her!"

"Mrs. Quarles never mentioned it," said Dulcey. He waved Finchley and de Ordas away. "I think it's time you realize, Benedict, that my patience is limited. I am a public servant and I take my duties seriously, if you do not. Now are you going to make sense? What did you mean by implying that there was another murder committed here? Who was killed, beside Gantredi? And Where's the body?"

McConaughy watched Jerry anxiously. Jerry sat back and said: "Frank Hamilton was killed."

"No, he wasn't, said Dulcey. "Hamilton powered out of town two weeks ago, after he tried to palm off that body in the North River."

"That's where you've gone wrong on

191

the case," Jerry said quietly. "Frank Hamilton didn't leave town, and he wasn't killed until tonight. He was killed right here, in this house."

Dulcey stared, icily furious, then turned to McConaughy.

"You can't deny that I've been patient with this man. I've given him every opportunity to clear himself." He waved a hand at Bakerman, "Take him into the kitchen and keep him there. I'll question all the others first. Maybe they'll make more sense."

★ ★ ★

His coat draped over a kitchen chair, Bakerman took the coffee pot from the stove and carefully poured into the three cups on the porcelain table. The wind, rising steadily, whimpered around the cornices of the old house. Isolated in the kitchen for the past twenty minutes, Jerry controlled his impatience with difficulty as he watched the tall, middle-aged cop.

"That Dulcey," said Bakerman. "He reminds me of my wife; always wants to do the thinking for me. Takes credit for everything and never gives a guy a chance to get ahead." He waved an aggrieved spoon. "He never even said a word when we brought in Dykes and Chalett with you. Any other time, he'd have sent a full squad with riot guns to pick up George, and here Peasey and me did it all by ourselves."

Pease drank his coffee with noisy sucking sounds.

"Dulcey stinks," he said.

Jerry said: "Well, what are you going to do about it?"

All the time he had been shut off in the kitchen, he had talked steadily to the two cops. He omitted nothing of the night's happenings. He directed his talk to Bakerman, judging the tall man to be the more intelligent of the two. Pease still regarded him with dark, feral eyes. His concluding remarks were a bitter indictment of Dulcey's methods, and now he waited anxiously for Bakerman's reaction.

Bakerman was thinking of his wife and his years as a second-grade detective. He looked weary. Jerry went on:

"Dulcey doesn't know anything about Polders being one of Frank's old pals. If I give it to him, he'll claim he sweated it out of me and get all the credit, which really belongs to you."

"That Dulcey," Bakerman said again.

Pease licked his lips. He regarded Jerry with eyes like those of a mouse peeking from its hole.

"Where did you say you saw Frankie's body?"

"Upstairs, on the third floor."

"And nobody's seen it but you?"

"As far as I know," said Jerry.

The two cops exchanged glances. Bakerman said slowly: "One of us ought to pick up Polders, though. He might skip."

"Yeah," Pease nodded.

Bakerman said: "You go, Peasey. I'll look upstairs."

Pease was suddenly alarmed. "Hell, no, not me. Dulcey would singe my tail-feathers."

"How are we going to work it, then? One of us has to go there," Bakerman said, heavily patient.

Pease put down his coffee with exasperation, and stood up. He glared at Jerry. "But suppose this guy's lyin', Harvey? Then I'll be seein' you out on a beat in the Bronx."

Bakerman took his police revolver from his hip pocket and leveled it at Jerry, pretended to cock it with his thumb, and said: "Bang." His face was without expression. "If he's lying, Peasey, we'll both be seeing him in the morgue."

They quit the apartment by way of the kitchen door and reached Harvey Street from the alley. Jerry hoped fervently that Frank Hamilton's body was where he had left it; but his main interest was in searching the third floor for any trace of Stephanie. The green neon sign over Ernie's Bar was dark and silent for the night as they reached the sidewalk. Pease hunched his shoulders in the rain and said: "Well, so long," and walked off. Bakerman prodded Jerry with his gun. "Lead on, son."

The door in the alley between the darkened pet shop and the liquor store was still unlocked. The big cop sprayed his flashlight suspiciously up the narrow shaft of stairs in the rear of No. 16 Waverly Walk.

"Up here?" he asked.

Jerry nodded. "I think Hamilton used this third floor for business contacts other than those we know about. Mrs. Quarles thinks a Julian Street lived up here, but she's never seen him — in fact, no one saw him, for the simple reason that Street doesn't exist and they've always seen Frank Hamilton. I didn't find any clothes or anything else to show that a Julian Street actually lived here. Besides, there's a telephone on the third floor that's an extension to the one in Hamilton's old apartment. That proves a connection, doesn't it?"

Bakerman thought it proved a connection, indeed. The door at the head of the steep staircase was still open like the street door. Jerry stepped into the familiar mustiness of the rooms, remembering his other visit and the crack on the head someone had given him. The rooms were dark now, and he didn't recall turning off the lights the other time. He hesitated, frowning, and Bakerman prodded him with the gun.

"You first," said the cop. "Where's the body?"

Jerry's stomach was tied into knots, worrying over what had happened to Stephanie. If she, too, was a victim of that sunburst spike . . . His palms went sweaty at the thought. He led Bakerman through all the other rooms in the apartment, opening closet doors and going down on hands and knees to peer behind the furniture. There was no sign of the girl.

"In the bedroom," he said finally.

Bakerman muttered: "Why didn't you say so in the first place?" He sprayed his light into the disheveled bedroom and growled a curse before turning back to Jerry.

"It's Frankie Hamilton, all right." he added casually: "And that's all I wanted to see. I guess we'd better go."

"Where to now?" Jerry asked.

"Something tells me," Bakerman drawled, "that you're going straight into the calaboose."

13

JERRY stretched out comfortably on his cot and listened to the muted traffic sounds from beyond the barred window of his cell. It was just three o'clock in the afternoon, and the night of rain was replaced by the clear skies of a windy October day. Inside the jail, however, it still smelled damp.

He felt refreshed after twelve hours in the cell. On a tray were the remains of a meal he had ordered from outside — shrimp cocktail in a silver ice bowl, tenderloin steak with fried onions, and a tossed green salad. Coffee still steamed gently in a little silver pot. He had charged the dinner to the *Globe*, and felt content.

Rolling over on his side, he moodily considered the collection of caricatures he had made of the people involved in the Waverly Walk murders. The brief line drawings mirrored, in Jerry's own perspective, the basic features of each one — with here an elongated Pinocchio nose, there a Mephistophelean leer. A vaguely disturbing idea floated nebulously in the back of his mind. But he couldn't capture it. Turning away from the scattered cartoons, he gazed thoughtfully through the barred window. He could see a rectangle of blue sky and hear the pleasant bluster of the wind as it whipped and tumbled between the tall buildings.

After a while keys rattled in his cell block. Hoots of derision from other prisoners marked the jailer's progress as he neared Jerry's door and peered in.

"They're fixin' papers to let you out," the guard announced. "And this guy wants to see you."

It was Sparling, the *Globe*'s dour rewrite man. Jerry yawned and sat up on the cot.

"'Fond words have oft been spoke to

thee, Sleep!'" He scowled at Sparling's thin figure. "That's Wordsworth. I was beginning to think I'd never get out of this dungeon." He turned to the jailer. "Did you ever hear of the Prisoner of Chillon? Or the Count of Monte Cristo, varlet?"

"I don't know about this Chillon clink," said the guard. "But you got treated good by the rules here."

Sparling said: "We'll have to wait until the papers go through. It won't take more than a few minutes."

The jailer went away. Jerry said: "I thought McConaughy was going to let me languish here forever."

"He ought to," Sparling said with prim disapproval. "How does it feel to be a bridegroom?"

"A what?"

"What was the idea of marrying that girl?"

"Which girl?" Jerry asked.

Sparling looked revolted. "Were you drunk? Don't you even remember?"

Jerry frowned. "Oh, *that* girl! Is that

what everybody thinks? That I really married her?"

"Well, didn't you?" Sparling stepped carefully over the cartoons on the floor and sat down on the cot as Jerry cleared them away. "Dulcey only booked you as a material witness, that's why you get out so soon. Anyway, you're off the case and back on editorials." Sparling watched Jerry stuff the caricatures into his pocket. "After all the things you did, you should consider yourself lucky. I could think of a few morals charges that could keep you here longer, if you like."

"Did Dulcey find that girl yet?" Jerry asked.

"Everybody thinks you've got her. Your phone's been ringing all day about it. Lots of people want to know about Mrs. Benedict."

"Mrs. Ben — " Jerry paused. "What people?"

"Mostly it was a little Cuban named Rodriquez. Said he had some information for you, about de Ordas."

Jerry nodded, warmly grateful. "Did Rodriguez say where I could find him?"

"All he mentioned to identify himself was the Yellow Ox Tavern, in Havana." Sparling snickered. "Does he expect you to go to Cuba to solve this case?"

"The Yellow Ox Tavern," Jerry said grimly, "moved to Greenwich Village about ten years ago. When Fidel's gangsters moved into the original one, to be exact."

Sparling went on: "If I were McConaughy, I'd let you stew here a while. Some day you'll learn to play by the rules, Jerry. Marrying a girl just to get a story is pretty low."

Jerry said: "Yeah, but you didn't see this girl."

★ ★ ★

Ten minutes later he was free and out of jail. They paused on the sidewalk, searching for a cab. The wind boomed down the narrow street and tossed newspapers high in the air, bellied topcoats out and lifted women's skirts. A fat man chased his fedora as it rolled gaily across the intersection. Jerry watched a blonde go by, vainly trying to told on to her hat and dress at the same time. She succeeded with the hat only.

An urchin in a red sweater skipped across the sidewalk toward Jerry and Sparling. Across the front of the sweater was the legend, The Belvedere Bats. His freckled face looked impatient as he tugged at Jerry's sleeve.

"You Mr. Benedict, mister?"

Jerry said: "Hi, Bat."

"Hi," said the boy. "Got a note for you." He searched through his corduroy trousers, delved inside the sweater for his shirt pocket, and brough out a crumpled piece of paper. "Lady said you'd gimme two bits for delivering."

"What lady?" Jerry asked.

"Lady what gimme the note for you."

Jerry unfolded the scrap of paper and

read it swiftly. The paper was delicate lavender, none too subtly scented; the script was fine and spidery, in green ink. It read: *Jerry — If you want to find out about your wife and maybe learn where she is, come see me as soon as you can at the Nugget Club..* The note was signed *Patti*. Jerry thought a moment about Patti Duggan, then put the note away and gave the urchin a dollar. "Go buy yourself a belfry, bat," he said.

"T'anks," said the boy.

He skipped away. A cab slid to the curb in response to Sparling's impatient signals and Jerry climbed in after him, said, "The Globe Building, and don't spare the horses." Then he looked quickly at the cab driver's identification, but it wasn't Shultz, and he leaned back with a sigh of relief. The cab pulled away smoothly, turned the corner, and just made the green traffic light.

A small coupé, motor roaring, suddenly pulled up from behind and swept past. Jerry had no chance to see the men in the other car. The cab driver suddenly yelled in alarm and yanked wildly at the wheel. Jerry grabbed Sparling and hurled him to the floor of the cab. A shotgun thundered deafeningly and glass tinkled as the side windows were blasted to fragments. The cab hit the curb, blew out two tires, and plowed into the window of a delicatessen store. A shower of canned goods from the window display clattered on the side of the cab.

The coupé roared around the corner and vanished.

Jerry picked himself up and stared at Sparling.

"You all right?"

"I — guess so." Sparling licked a bloody lip. "They tried to kill you, Jerry!"

"Well, either their luck was bad or their aim was pretty awful."

The cab driver was groaning. He had a cut over his forehead, and his eyes were wild with anguish as he surveyed the debris. A small crowd gathered.

The delicatessen owner stood in his doorway and wrung his hands. His wife was screaming for the police as Jerry crawled painfully out of the twisted door of the taxi.

"You handle it, Sparling," he said.

"Me?"

"McConaughy wants to see me, doesn't he?" He spotted a traffic cop pounding down the sidewalk. "Make my excuses."

Pushing through the little crowd, he left Sparling surrounded by the angry cab driver, the delicatessen owner, and interested bystanders. There was no sign of the coupé. Jerry smoothed his hat into shape and leaned into the wind, walking casually past the running patrolman at the outer edge of the crowd.

Nobody stopped him.

14

MCCONAUGHY said: "You cost us a mint of money, Jerry."

The fat editor of the *Globe* sat behind his desk like a sadly disillusioned Asiatic deity, shaking his curly head. He pursed his little mouth and looked at Jerry without much friendliness.

Jerry said indignantly: "Well, I didn't ask to be shot at, did I? If I'm willing to die for the dear old *Globe*, I don't see why you should complain."

Bakerman said: "Well, you came through it all right, Jerry, and that's what matters." The tall detective sat quietly on a golden-oak office chair. "You have any idea who they were?"

"I never saw them," Jerry said. "I hit the deck too fast."

"You suppose they were George Chalett's men?"

"Could be. Nobody ever threw a gun on Chalett like I did, last night. I imagine he's peeved. With him, it's a question of upholding his professional reputation. Or maybe de Ordas finally recognized me from the Havana days."

McConaughy rumbled: "Bakerman suggests that it will be better all around if you worked with him until this business is cleared up. He's on his own time now."

"Thanks," Jerry protested, "but I don't need a nurse maid."

"Neverthelesss, that's an order from upstairs."

Distantly from beyond the pebbled glass office doors came rumble of presses putting out an extra edition. Bakerman hiked up his wrinkled trousers and regarded Jerry curiously.

"Where do you suppose that girl is?" he asked.

"I wish I knew," said Jerry glumly. "I'm scared to death, thinking of what could happen to her. Hasn't anybody checked her home address?"

McConaughy pawed papers on his desk. "It's a Village apartment, Smith Street, Number 55A. But she hasn't been seen since yesterday morning. She's disappeared, all right."

Bakerman said: "What about that concertina?"

Jerry shrugged. "I think Hamilton's money was in it. I guess the girl has it now."

"Think she blew town with it?"

"No. She's not that kind of a girl. She's either hiding somewhere, scared witless, or Finchley and de Ordas got her stowed away somewhere. Those two were with her when I left." He frowned. "But why should they have been hanging around when you fellows got there, if they snatched her?"

McConaughy said uneasily: "Look, Jerry, you're officially through with this story. Maybe you'd better forget the whole thing."

Jerry said tightly: "Fine thing. I get slugged, tossed in the can, and shot at. I'm considered a destroyer of morals and a sex fiend. But don't think I'm going to quietly fold my tent and steal back to the editorial page without settling this first."

Bakerman's voice was placid.

"Maybe you'd like to know what we've discovered, anyway. We checked everybody, but take Stephanie first: she works as a model for the Fairbanks Company, but they say she hasn't reported in for the past two days. She's often been irregular in assignments before, too. The landlord of her house on Smith Street gives us no help at all — says she's quiet, respectable, and had no male callers. Yet she sure is in this up to her neck. She left Dulcey's office yesterday and had plenty of time to get to Waverly Walk, kill Gantredi, and get back to the *Globe* and pretend to just learn of the apartment ad."

"She wouldn't kill anybody," Jerry said.

McConaughy spread his fat hands. "Well, where is she, then? If the money is in that concertina, and she's missing now, then she either swiped it, or she's met with — uh — foul play."

"What about Finchley?" Jerry demanded.

"No alibies at all. His secretary said he left work at lunch time and never returned. Finchley himself says he walked around in the rain all afternoon, worrying about business."

"And de Ordas?"

McConaughy coughed behind his fat hand.

"The FBI will take care of de Ordas. They know all about him, Jerry. It's a diplomatic matter, though."

"What about his alibi?" Jerry insisted.

"He hasn't any. And Chalett hasn't been picked up since Dulcey released him last night. He's probably holed up somewhere."

Jerry shook his head. "Well, he's still in touch with his pals. He sent them after me to blast me, didn't he?"

"Dulcey will take care of Chalett," said McConaughy.

"If Chalett doesn't take care of me

first," Jerry said glumly. "That man scares me."

Bakerman said: "We questioned Wanda Dykes, too. She claims she was at a cocktail party when Gantredi was killed, and that she went straight home from Waverly Walk and had no opportunity to kill Hamilton. We're checking the party to see if she was really there. The clerk at her hotel says that she got back later than she claims at 7:20 last night — which still gives her time to kill Hamilton.

"Apple and Polders look like a good bet, too. Since Polders once belonged to Frankie's mob, he wouldn't mind cutting himself a chunk of pie, especially when the pie practically falls in his lap with Frankie landing in his hospital. But Polders' staff says he was at his office until 6:45, which rules out the chance that he killed Gantredi, anyway. The M.E. says Gantredi died at about 5:30, and Hamilton about an hour later. So you see, none of this mob of doublecrossers has an alibi, anyway."

McConaughy waved pudgy hands. "This isn't getting us anywhere. The thing to do is to find that Stephanie dame."

"And the concertina," Bakerman nodded.

Both men stared at Jerry.

"Well, don't look at me," he protested. "I haven't got her in my back pocket."

Bakerman said: "You sure you didn't arrange to meet her somewhere?"

Jerry looked pained. "I like that girl. She's involved, yes, but I'm betting my nickels on her innocence."

McConaughy said: "Well, Bakerman just wanted to ask. I told you, Jerry, he wants to work with you on his own time. I suggest that you cooperate with him."

Jerry shrugged. He thought of the note he had received from Patti Duggan, but he didn't say anything about it. Abruptly he delved into his sock, took off his shoe, turned the sock inside out and placed the two scraps of dark celluloid on McConaughy's desk.

"There's something you ought to look into."

"What is it?" McConaughy asked.

"Microfilm. There was a roll of it hidden in the socket of the mirror frame. That's where the murder spike came from, in case Dulcey hasn't figured it out yet. The murderer's got the roll of film now, but maybe we can find out from these scraps what Hamilton's business deals were. My guess is that these are part of his records."

"I'll check," Bakerman said and pocketed the scraps.

Jerry said: "Does anyone know just how much money is supposed to be in that concertina?"

"About four hundred grand," Bakerman said drily. "Hamilton collected surplus cash from the big guns in the rackets for investment in real estate and legitimate businesses, and he also had de Ordas' loot in his mitts when things began to happen."

Jerry whistled. "Good for a couple

of murders more. Maybe he planned to skip with all the loot."

"And was slugged before he got started," McConaughy nodded. "Obviously de Ordas and the others want their cash back — as much of it as they can find. Gantredi probably got in the way by discovering the cash, and that makes his murder almost incidental."

"Not to Gantredi," Jerry said wryly.

Bakerman said: "Anyway, this whole thing goes back to when Hamilton was first slugged. The M.E. found a bad concussion, maybe two weeks old. Frankie was a walking dead man when he was stabbed. I figure he was slugged because he was going to talk to the authorities about the black markets. He told the court he was ready to reform and settle down and be a family man. We'll find the murderer when we find the one who put that lump on Frankie's skull."

"Did he have a family?" Jerry frowned. He shrugged and looked thoughtful. "Right now, anyway, it seems more important to me to find out about Johnny Lisbon. How was he tied in with Frank Hamilton? If Hamilton framed it to look as if he himself was dead, why pick on one of his own boys to provide a corpse for him? He could have found some bum in a smoke joint that nobody would miss. Why kill his own man, if he had ideas of escaping the law by pretending to be dead?"

"That's just it," Bakerman sighed. "We don't know if Hamilton was slugged first, or if Johnny Lisbon was killed first. They both disappeared about two weeks ago. But Lisbon tied in with Hamilton long ago, in the drug syndicate days; He was about ten years younger than Hamilton, with a mind like a snake. He came into the organization just after Queen Madge disappeared."

"Queen Madge?"

"She ran Hamilton's narcotics ring for him, in the days before Frank got out of the rackets and began his career as 'The Investor' for the other syndicate leaders," Bakerman said. "A fabulous lady, she was. You wouldn't remember her Jerry, but she still shows up in the Sunday supplements. She was Hamilton's woman — maybe married to him, maybe not. She was nuts about him; she acted like a slave when he was around. Some artist guy who wanted to paint her once told me she reminded him of some Greek statue, by some Polly-Whichever."

"By Policlitus," Jerry said absently. "What happened to her?"

"I never saw her myself, and nobody ever got a picture of her, either. She was never picked up or mugged, anyway." Bakerman snapped his fingers. "She disappeared — like that. Nobody knows about it. It was twenty years ago, anyway, and I figure she's been dead long since."

"Did Lisbon know her?"

"Maybe. But he came in after Queen Madge disappeared. Lisbon took over her chores for Hamilton. He was a pretty snotty boy in those days. I remember once when Hamilton was standing trial for some gang murder, Lisbon stood up in court and gave him the alibi he needed."

"Then Lisbon saved Hamilton from the chair once?"

"Sure, by perjury."

Jerry stood up. "I'm betting the solution to Johnny Lisbon's murder will answer every angle in this case."

He was almost to the door when McConaughy said sharply:

"Wait a minute, Jerry. I'm fond of you, boy. You're in this too deep to quit now, I know that; but you'll work with Bakerman from here on out. You're not to go anywhere or do anything without him. Suppose even something simple like a broken finger happened to you, boy? Where would your work be then? You've got to watch your hands like a musician, and if Chalett's boys rough you up — "

Jerry paused and pushed his hat back

on his unruly red hair. He grinned at Bakerman.

"You might come in handy at that," he said.

Bakerman said somberly: "Maybe you don't see the setup, Jerry. These people are desperate, and they're out to get that dough any way they can. And they think you have it."

"Me?"

"You or the girl," Bakerman nodded. "They'll be looking for you both, and they won't mind a workout on either of you."

* * *

Sparling knocked on the office door, thrust his head inside, and said: "Phone for you, Benedict. On your desk."

"Be back in a moment," Jerry said to McConaughy.

He stepped into the city room with Sparling. The dour rewrite man removed a handkerchief from his eye and revealed a puffy, blackened orb.

Jerry whistled appreciatively.

"How'd you get that?" he asked. "In the taxi?"

"It was the delicatessen man's wife," Sparling said. He winced at the memory. "I tried to tell her the accident wasn't our fault, and she said I was drunk and socked me with a salami. And I've never touched liquor in my life."

"Now you see what it gets you," Jerry said.

He went on to his desk and picked up the telephone. His hands trembled a little as he thought of Stephanie and what Bakerman had said.

"Jerry?" It was a woman's voice, but it wasn't Stephanie. "This is Patti Duggan, Jerry. Did you get my note?"

"A bat fluttered over and dropped it with a ghastly screech," he said. "But I thought you called it quits yesterday."

Patti Duggan's voice was a soft, frightened whisper. "I'm too stupid to know what's good for me, I guess. I want to find out who killed Johnny. I figure I owe it to him. He was pretty good to me."

"Where do you want me to meet you?" Jerry asked.

"We'll have to be careful." Patti's voice was almost inaudible. "If you can come to the Nugget Club in Brooklyn . . . "

"What time?"

"Make it by eight this evening. I'll have some information you can use, Jerry. But come in through the stage door. The doorman will let you in."

Jerry said anxiously: "Now wait a minute, Patti. If you know anything, spill it now. Don't keep it until later."

"I can't. Not over the phone. 'Bye."

The receiver clicked drily. Jerry jiggled the hook for a moment, then slammed the telephone down with a scowl. The wind made the big windows shake and rattle. Long shafts of golden sunlight slanted across the street. It was just four o'clock. He glanced at McConaughy's office door, but it was still closed. Worry over Stephanie made him follow a quick decision. He walked over to the fire-escape exit and made his way quickly down to the main floor and the street. What he wanted to do, he decided, could be done better without Bakerman. Especially if Stephanie was in serious trouble and needed help.

15

NUMBER 55A Smith Street was a narrow blue house with a court in the rear, and a tailor shop next door. The wind blew ashes and scraps of paper high in the air over the narrow, twisting street. A black coupé was parked across from the tailor shop, pointing in the same direction as Jerry walked when he left the subway station. He paused as he came abreast of the rear fender and abruptly took two steps backward as he recognized Lieutenant Dulcey sitting stolidly behind the wheel of the coupé.

He wondered if the smudge-eyed Pease were upstairs in Stephanie Farley's apartment, and didn't like the idea. He turned his back abruptly toward Dulcey, in the car, and there was no alarm. A dilapidated sign on the brick wall of the alley bore the legend, ADAM'S GARDEN COURT — NO VACANCIES. Jerry pushed on up the alley.

The courtyard was shrouded in dusky shadows. There was a dry concrete fountain supported by rococo cupids, a dispirited maple tree, and iron-railed balconies of pseudo-Spanish style adorned with Moorish columns. No one was about. An arched doorway opened into the back entrance to Adam's Court. The first door was ajar, and dim light flickered within. Jerry knocked tentatively on the panels and pushed the door all the way open.

"Go drown yourself," said a man's voice.

Jerry blinked in the dim light. The man was wearing a daubed artist's smock and he was painting a canvas by the light of two smoky, guttering candles.

"I beg your pardon," Jerry said.

The man had a stringy beard that matched his lank hair. His eyes were weary. "One might as well try creative art at the information booth in Grand Central Station," he sighed. "Go away!"

Jerry said: "Why don't you pull up the shades? You could see better."

"I *like* candlelight," said the bearded man. "I get the proper texture for my colors. This will be entitled, 'Omelet the Morning Before.'"

"Have it your way," said Jerry. "So it's an omelet. I'm only looking for someone, that's all."

"I'm looking for an omelet," said the artist. "The name is Sylvester Johnson. No doubt you've heard of me. Have you got any money?"

Jerry put a dollar bill on the table.

"I'm looking for a Miss Stephanie Farley," Jerry said. "I understand she lives here."

Sylvester Johnson pocketed the dollar bill and blew out the candles. The room was plunged into thick gloom. He said: "She isn't here, but thanks for the dollar, friend. You can tell your grandchildren that you helped subsidize the great Sylvester Johnson one day."

"Well, which is her apartment?" Jerry asked.

"Third floor. The green door."

Jerry followed him out into the corridor. There were voices from the second floor landing, loud in argument.

"Did you come here to discuss . . . ?" asked the man petulantly.

The woman's voice was sharp. "Yes, I came to discuss!"

"Do you always discuss by kicking the door down?"

"I did *not* kick the door down!"

"That proves it," said the man triumphantly. "You didn't come here to discuss. You came here to beat me!"

The sound of a blow made Jerry wince. He started up to the third floor, and a door was flung open behind him. The man's voice followed the woman who came out. "Bernice, if you ever hit me again . . . " The woman gestured in disgust, and glared at Jerry on the steps above her. She couldn't have weighed more than eighty pounds. She put her childish hands on equally childish hips.

"Man or beast?" she demanded.

"Argh!" said Jerry.

"Then let me pass, beast," said the little woman.

He followed her upstairs to the top landing.

"Are you looking for someone?" she asked curiously.

She held the door open for him. Evidently Bernice was a student of sculpture. The room was long, with an extraordinarily high ceiling, a wide studio couch, a Japanese screen, and a heavy table heaped with modeling clay. A pair of nylon stockings hung over the wash stand. On every available horizontal inch of space rested grotesque heads, torsos, and geometrical forms that defied analysis. The largest one stood on the modeling table, sprouting out of the mass of clay. Jerry stared at it.

Little Bernice said: "That's called

'Wings of Night Over a Paper Box Factory.' Do you like it?"

Jerry started to reply, then recalled Sylvester Johnson and nodded. "It's very pretty," he said weakly.

"It stinks," said Bernice. She examined the skinned knuckles of her tiny hand. She had a spray of freckles across her tilted nose. "Whom are you looking for?"

"Miss Farley," Jerry said.

The little woman picked up a bread knife from beside the wash bowl and pointed it at Jerry's tall figure.

"You get the hell out of here," she said, "Why don't you cops heckle somebody your own size! Pick on me, why don't you?"

"I'm not a cop," Jerry said. "Honest."

She kept the knife in her hand. "Then what do you want with Steve? What's she done, anyway?"

"She's in trouble," Jerry said, "and I want to help her. You see, we were married yesterday, and we were looking for an apartment — "

Bernice began to glow. "Oh, my dear boy. My *dear* boy! So you're Steve's husband! I read about it in the newspapers."

"About our marriage?"

"About the murder. Poor Steve!"

"Look," Jerry said desperately, "she's in danger, and I'm trying to find her so I can help her. The cops don't even know I'm here; I came in the back way."

"Did you see Sylvester?" she asked. "He *really* stinks. That candlelight theory of his is strictly for the birds. That's why he leaves the door open — he wants people to think he's eccentric."

"About Steve," Jerry said. "Do you know where she is?"

Bernice frowned. "Nope."

"Are you sure?"

There came a thunderous knocking on the door. A man's burly voice, the someone Jerry had heard on the second floor, came plaintively through the panel.

230

"Bernice, *chérie*. I wish to be forgiven."

"Go to hell!" Bernice called.

"But I've come to discuss!"

Bernice put away her bread knife, looked at Jerry. "Oh, God, you'd better get out of here. That's Jefferson. He'll go berserk if he finds another man in my room."

Jerry felt bewildered. "How can I get out?"

"Through the balcony window. You can get back to the stairs through Steve's apartment."

There was more thunderous knocking on the door as Jerry raised the tall window and stepped over the sill into the windy dusk. Bernice followed him and said:

"I almost forgot. She telephoned me this morning."

"She *what*?" Jerry yelled.

"She telephoned. Said you should meet her — " Bernice turned away. "Jefferson, *wait*! She slammed the window shut, shrugged her tiny

231

shoulders, and went away toward the door. Jerry abruptly ducked out of sight. He didn't want to be embroiled with Jefferson.

The sky to the west was a riot of orange and purple color. Jerry moved down on the balcony.

Steve's windows sported bright red curtains with horizontal yellow stripes. The sash went up noiselessly, and Jerry swung inside and stood blinking into the gloom. There was a faint scent of perfume in the air, a lingering breath of femininity that was like a forgotten melody. There was a bright kitchen table, a china cupboard painted a gay blue with stenciled swans, a row of orange dishes, and a bowl of apples on the table.

"Nice girl," Jerry murmured.

He parted the curtains to the living room, took in the simple, brightly colored furniture, a work table on which were posed three manikins in miniature dresses, and a small Governor Winthrop secretary. There were no signs of disorder. He wondered if the cops had left anything useful, and turned to examine the secretary. There were no personal letters in the pigeonholes: only a few bills, neatly documented, a memorandum book with all the past dated pages torn out, a leatherette address book. He picked up, flipped through the pages; most of the names were strange to him; a few he recognized as model agencies.

Under the 'L's' were three names listed: Lamont's Agency, someone named Lucinda Lane, and then the notation, *J.L. — re br cert, AL2-2250*. Jerry looked around for a telephone and found none. He wished he had time to go back and question Bernice, next door. If Stephanie had telephoned her this morning and left a message for him, it meant she was free, at any rate. He shook his head, and looked into the bathroom.

The medicine chest contained the usual cold cream jars, a stick of mascara, bath salt, two toothbrushes.

He pulled the shower curtains idly aside, and then abruptly stiffened as a key tickled the hall door.

The lock clicked and a footfall that was a mere ghost of a sound came from the living room. Jerry stood motionless, holding his breath. There came another stealthy step and the rattle of papers from the living room.

Jerry wished he had a gun.

It wasn't a cop, he decided; a cop wouldn't be so quiet. He stepped into the next room.

"Don't move!" he rapped.

There came a gasp from the shadowy figure bending over the open desk. Then he suddenly whirled, and a paperweight flashed by Jerry's head, thudded into a chair beside him. Jerry left his feet in a long, diving tackle that hit the man just above the knees and brought him down with a crash.

A fist flailed furiously, queerly womanish, against Jerry's chest. Nails raked painfully across his face. Jerry got his fingers under the man's necktie, bunched it tightly, and yanked him to his feet, lifting him with his fist under his chin until the man was on tiptoe.

"Well, well, well, Mr. Finchley," Jerry said. He sounded savage and satisfied.

Mr. Finchley gasped. "You're choking me!" His steel-rimmed spectacles dangled loosely from one sharply pointed, elfin ear. "Lemme go!" he whispered.

Jerry let him down a little. "You've saved me a lot of trouble looking for you, Oliver."

The little man shrugged his coat straight. Jerry shoved him into the nearest chair. Finchley sat quivering.

Jerry said: "All right. Now tell me where she is."

"I don't know," Finchley whispered. "Honestly, I don't."

"I left her with you last night at Waverly Walk, didn't I?"

"Yes," Finchley nodded.

"What happened after I left?"

The little elf licked his lips. "I don't know."

"Maybe you don't understand how I feel about Stephanie Farley," Jerry said softly. He examined his fist with interest. "To hell with being polite, I say."

Finchley's words tumbled over each other.

"Now wait a minute. You don't understand, I really don't know where the girl is. I only wish I did know."

"What happened at Waverly Walk last night?"

"I — I ran away."

"But you were there when I got back," Jerry said.

"Yes. De Ordas forced me to come back. I — Miss Farley started to play that concertina, you remember. It didn't work very well and she left the living room and took the gun with her. I — I was rather panicky — knowing the police were about to arrive — so I ran out the front door."

"And why did you come back?"

"De Ordas chased after me and made me return. He insisted we face the police together, because they would get our names from the others, anyway. And when we walked back, the girl was gone. She had disappeared."

"And the concertina?"

"That was gone, too."

Jerry said: "What are you doing in her apartment now? What are you looking for?"

"Don't know," Finchley muttered. "I thought I might find some clue to her whereabouts in these rooms." He looked up anxiously. "If I knew where she was, I wouldn't come here, would I? I wouldn't have to, if I knew where she was."

Jerry hesitated, looking down at Finchley's pathetic, gnomelike figure. The apartment was almost completely dark now.

"Look here," said Finchley, gathering courage. "You're a newspaperman, and you are not naive. You have a reputation for being a clever young man. You know about the money I turned over to Frank Hamilton, don't you?"

"Suppose I do?"

"Well, you must understand my predicament, then. Why, I didn't even know Hamilton was still alive! The others knew," the little man added bitterly, "but I didn't. And he had all of my money. I'm desperate, I face complete ruin, unless I get that money back. After all, it belongs to me."

"It belongs to the Internal Revenue Service," Jerry said. "You've got a string of shady enterprises that make more money than you can legitimately account for, and you were using 'The Investor' to siphon it off. I don't think you'll see that money again."

Finchley's mouth tightened. "If you know where it is, I am willing to pay a handsome bonus for recovering it for me."

"How handsome?"

"Ten thousand," Finchley said.

Jerry rocked a little on his heels.

"That's not so handsome. That's a lot less than ten percent. Even a literary agent makes at least ten percent, and that's legalized robbery. This isn't even legal."

"Twenty thousand," said Finchley. He leaned forward eagerly. "Do you know where the money is?"

"Sure," said Jerry. "In the concertina. And the girl has that." His voice whetted itself on sharp anger. "And for two pins, I'd fix it so you wouldn't ever have to moo Worpheus again — "

There came a sudden sound of blows from the next apartment, then Bernice's voice shrilled: "Jefferson Blake, you beast! You didn't come here to discuss anything at all!"

"What's that all about?" Finchley whispered.

"It's a discussion," Jerry said.

There came another sharp rapping sound, this time from Stephanie's corridor door. It was followed by the scuffling of big shoes in the hallway, then a man's voice said:

"All right, Pease, get the key! If that screwball says two men came up here, they won't answer any knocks."

It was Lieutenant Dulcey.

"What's going on next door?" came Pease's voice.

"Not our business, dumbhead. Find that key!"

Finchley's face was white. Jerry suddenly yanked the little man to his feet and he burbled with fear, "See here, Benedict, I don't like being manhandled — "

"Shut up," said Jerry. "Those are cops outside."

"Cops?" Finchley went limp. "My word!"

The kitchen window was still open. Jerry pushed the little man over the sill to the balcony and tumbled out after him. Three floors down, the little rococo fountain was shrouded in deep darkness. A shaft of light made a flat yellow rectangle on the rough concrete floor of the balcony to his right. It came from Bernice's window. Jerry shoved the little man in that direction.

From inside Stephanie's apartment came the thud of the door as the detectives finally burst inside. Bernice's window wasn't locked. Jerry tumbled Finchley inside, pell-mell.

Bernice was standing near her modeling table, her little body trembling with suppressed rage. She spared a quick, disinterested glance at the two men climbing through her window, then returned her glare to the big man with her. He had a jet black beard and thick caterpillar brows; he wore a red-checked flannel shirt and corduroy trousers with a wide leather belt. His eyes were shiny with terror as he faced the little woman.

"Pardon us," Jerry said.

He pushed Finchley ahead toward the hall door.

"Who are you?" demanded the bearded man.

"Just innocent passersby," said Jerry. "Excuse us."

"Oh, yeah?" the big man bellowed.

His fear of Bernice and his need for vengeance focused on Jerry and Finchley. His big hands opened and closed with his fury.

Jerry said to the little woman: "Where did you say Stephanie told you I should meet her?"

"She didn't say exactly, dear boy. She just told me to tell you to stay in your own back yard."

Jerry frowned. "Did she sound all right?"

"Of course she sounded all right. Stop butting into my conversation."

"A thousand pardons," said Jerry. He started for the door again, but the bearded man blocked his way. "I demand an explanation. We will discuss this intrusion before you leave."

"All right," Jerry said. "Discuss it with Oliver."

He shoved the little man without warning at Bernice's hulking friend. Oliver tripped and slammed into the bearded man's stomach. They both hit the wall with a shock that made the building tremble. In the moment's respite, Jerry yanked open the hall door and peered out. The third-floor landing was deserted.

From inside Bernice's room came the sounds of a blow and Oliver Finchley's anguished wail of innocence. Jerry went down the back stairs three at a time. Nobody stopped him. On the first floor he passed Sylvester Johnson's doorway. It was still ajar. The lanky-haired artist was frying an omelet over a portable gas burner. He was cooking by candlelight, and he didn't look up as Jerry trotted softly by.

16

OUTSIDE, the sky had turned a violent purple, sprinkled with stars and tinged with a yellow afterglow in the west. A man in a brown hat leaned against a nearby fire hydrant, a cigarette drooping from his slack mouth. His eyes touched Jerry's briefly, then swung down to contemplate the pavement. Jerry turned up his coat collar against the bite of the wind and went up the street. It was too early to go to Brooklyn, and too late to go uptown to his rooms, although he hadn't been home for almost forty-eight hours. It was the man in the brown hat who helped him make up his mind.

Jerry paused. Again his eyes touched Jerry's and this time he smiled. The cigarette still drooped from his mouth as he plucked at Jerry's sleeve.

"Señor Benedict," he said softly. "*Buenas noches.*"

Looking at the little man, an old and bitter tension abruptly tightened in the pit of Jerry's stomach. Once again, in the whispered, lisping words, he remembered Castro's concentration camps.

"What is it?" he demanded harshly.

"It is nothing alarming, señor. I come from Rodriguez — of the Yellow Ox Tavern, in Havana. You were there, were you not, during the fighting? Rodriguez is now owner of the Yellow Ox, on Greenwich Street, as you know." The little man looked apologetic. "He has been trying to reach you all day. He sent me for you, if you be so kind as to accompany me."

"I know. How did you find me?"

The little man shrugged. "He reads in the papers of your difficulties. He knows you will be to that young lady's house, señor. I simply wait for you." The little man grinned now. He was missing several front teeth. "It is for your own good, Señor Benedict. You have been watched; and we observe the watcher, you might say."

"The *Seguridad*?" Jerry asked.

"They are here, as everywhere." The little man spat his hatred into the gutter. "Mother killers, devils. But you have your own difficulties, Señor Benedict, and Rodriguez offers help to you. If you will follow me?"

"*Vamos*," Jerry nodded.

He wished he had sought out Rodriguez before this. If anyone could tell him about de Ordas, it would be the fat Cuban. In the original fighting in the Sierra Madres, when Jerry was covering the story for the *Globe*, he had saved Rodriguez' life. Later, when the Cuban saw his revolution betrayed into Red hands, he had fled to establish the new Yellow Ox Tavern on Greenwich Street.

He followed his guide across Sixth Avenue and down a twisted little street to the café on the corner. It was a fragment of Old Havana, peopled by refugees from the Castro terror. The restaurant was full of long-forgotten smells, of wine and spices and fragrant cooking. There were only half a dozen men in the place. Jerry's guide smiled and nodded. The cigarette clinging to his lower lip was only half an inch long.

"Rodriguez will be here soon. You have time to dine, señor."

Jerry nodded. "I'll wait. But what's he got for me?"

"A pleasant surprise, señor. Be patient."

Jerry accepted a corner table from a dark, deep-bosomed girl, and ordered *arroz con pollo* with a bottle of white wine. Rodriguez' cooking was no worse for the years gone by since the Cuban days. The waitress curled up in a rear booth, with a guitar and filled the air with quaint, lilting melodies.

Rodriguez appeared ten minutes later. He came at a waddling gait, beaming, and extended a hard hand.

"Señor Jerry. A pleasure, indeed."

He was short and stout, with alert eyes in a round, dark face. A scar crossed his cheekbone and vanished into his thick, gray hair just above his left ear. "I hope you don't mind my sending for you, Jerry."

"I should have thought of coming here myself."

"It is six months since you visited my café."

"My apologies. I've been busy."

"Yes. You fight with the pen now, not with the sword."

"Our enemies have become shadows," Jerry said.

"Dangerous shadows, *amigo*." Rodriguez leaned forward over the table; his hands were scrupulously clean. "I've been reading the papers, and the case you are working on involves a countryman — let him be damned in ten thousand hells, the Red pig."

"He says he's an Argentine now," Jerry said.

"Castro's arm, helped by Russia and China, reaches over all of South

America. His agents are very busy, like rats gnawing away at a granary. Our Señor de Ordas, having been in the S.P.S. and then, like the thief he truly is, betraying even the Castroites for profit, is a sick man with the lust for blood. It is a sickness he will not be rid of until he is dead."

Jerry met the dark eyes of the fat man across the table.

He said quietly: "Is de Ordas going to die?"

"I think so, *si*."

Jerry said: "I want to talk to him first."

"It can be arranged. That is why you are here, *amigo*." Rodriguez poured from the bottle of white wine. Abruptly he began to laugh, a short, fat little belly laugh that shook him from stem to stern. He leaned forward, wheezing a little.

"Have you found your wife yet?"

"She's not my wife," said Jerry. "Not yet."

"Ah, the newspapers were in error." The fat man smiled. The waitress in the corner changed tempo on her guitar and the air was sprinkled with sad little notes, each as plaintive as a tear. Rodriguez went on: "Yet you are fond of this girl."

"Very fond," Jerry admitted. "She's headstrong and I'm not sure she knows what she's getting into. That's why I want to see de Ordas. He was with her last, when she disappeared."

"You will see him," Rodriguez said.

"When?"

"Now."

Jerry half stood up. The candlelight made his red hair flame. "Now? Where is he? What's so funny?"

Rodriguez was laughing loudly, a rippling chuckle that made his belly heave. Tears sprang to his dark eyes.

"Where is he, you ask? He is here, Señor Jerry! He has come to us for protection against the *Seguridad*!"

Jerry stared into the face of the fat man's amusement.

"Here?" he whispered. "To you? Is he mad?"

"Mad with fear. You can see him for yourself."

"I wouldn't miss this," Jerry murmured, "for the world."

Following Rodriguez, he passed through the little restaurant to the back door. The man in the brown hat was lounging in the corridor. He bobbed his head and closed the door behind them. The sound of the girl's guitar was abruptly cut off. They all went up creaking stairs, lighted by a flickering gas jet, to the third floor. Their shadows were long and gaunt before them on the peeling paper walls. Another man was seated in a chair, tilted back against the banister, reading a Spanish newspaper by the light of a second gas jet. He started to rise, and Rodriquez waved him back to his comfortable perch.

"Secure?" Rodriguez asked, in Spanish.

"He does not wish to leave," said

the second guard, and grinned. "He offered me much money, Rodriguez."

Rodriguez grunted. "He offered me more, I assure you. He sees only wealth and power as the prime mover of all things, and thinks we will cast aside the years of exile and war for some paltry dollars. What a fool he is, when you come down to it!"

Their shadows danced ahead of them into the front room. It was a wide room, with two tall windows overlooking the street. There was an old iron bed and two worn, brown Morris chairs. Thin yellow curtains covered the windows. The room was filled with deep shadows. De Ordas, tall and gaunt, was at the corner window, peering into the street.

"Señor," Rodriguez said softly.

The tall man whirled. Even in the dimness, Jerry could see the change that fear had worked in him. His face was haunted. There was even a change in the way his clothing hung on his six-foot frame. His hands made pale arabesques in the gloom, as he gestured to Jerry.

"Where did he come from?"

"I sent for him," Rodriguez explained. "It is a little matter he wishes to discuss with you."

"A little matter of murder," Jerry added.

De Ordas contemplated him with hooded, suspicious eyes. "I did not kill anyone." He swung in dismissal to Rodriguez' fat little figure. "They know I am here. You must have told them."

"Who?"

"My enemies," de Ordas said harshly.

"I thought they were your friends."

De Ordas palmed the air. "They think I wanted that money — for myself."

"Didn't you?" Rodriguez asked mildly.

De Ordas wet his lips, turned back to the window. "Those two men — twenty minutes, they've been out there."

Jerry looked down at the street corner. It was like peering down on a stage from a box seat. In the light of the street lamp could be seen two men, motionless against the brick wall of the opposite house, their faces shadowed under their hat brims. They were looking up at the third-floor windows. Rodriguez made a clicking sound with his tongue, pulled the blind down, and drew de Ordas back. For a moment the room was in deep darkness, then a match sputtered and a gas jet in the wall flickered to life.

"Sit down," Rodriguez said.

De Ordas sank into a seat. He seemed to gain some confidence from Jerry's presence. He said softly:

"Mistakes I have made, yes — but you do not know them, Rodriguez!"

"*I* don't know them?" Rodriguez smiled. It was an entirely mirthless smile. "I spent two years in your filthy camps, did I not?"

"Of that I know nothing. But if so, then you must be aware of their methods. They will hunt me down, shoot without question."

"You would be lucky. No questions! Ah, how they loved to question me! With castor oil, and a whip, and other little niceties."

De Ordas didn't seem to hear. "You will give me a chance, though. I can give you much information on their plans, how they work, who their agents are."

Jerry said: "Why didn't you go to the police for protection?"

De Ordas spread his hands. "The police? To admit that I planned to take the money out of the country? Then they would surely think I killed Hamilton."

"Didn't you?"

"Of course not. I did not even know he was still alive. The others knew," he said bitterly, "but I didn't."

"Did Finchley kill him?"

"Of that I know nothing."

"Where is the girl, Steve Farley? You and Finchley were with her last, weren't you?"

De Ordas shrugged. "True. But she

disappeared while I was out of the building. I have not seen her since."

Jerry said: "You remember I left the house, when all the lights went out?"

"*Si*, I remember."

"Where were you at the time?"

"Outside, watching. I saw the lights go out."

"Did you see Finchley in the lobby?"

"I saw him go into the house. Then you came out, Señor Benedict, and a moment later, the girl followed. You went around the corner. The girl turned and came back. You see, I did not expect either of you to spend the night there, and I hoped to make one last search. It was my only hope. If I found the money — "

"Then your pals would forgive you, sure."

"They accept success only. Failure means I betrayed them."

"How long did you stand out there after the girl came back?"

De Ordas considered. "Five minutes, perhaps ten. No one else come out."

"Did anyone go in?"

"No. I went inside afterward. Mr. Finchley was talking to the girl, in the lobby. We all went into the apartment, then you came down."

"Did you see Mrs. Quarles at any time?"

"*Si*. She came up from the cellar while I was in the lobby and went directly upstairs."

"How did she act?"

"One does not know what she thinks about."

"Did she seem upset at the time?"

"It is difficult to say. She went directly upstairs, then you came down and advised us that she had found Gantredi's body. After you went out, Finchley began to behave most strangely."

"You mean he was frightened?"

"Yes."

"And you weren't?"

"I thought only to search for the money."

"With the police coming?"

"There were still a few minutes. You understand, I *had* to have that money. It is a matter of life and death to me. I thought Finchley came back because he knew where it might be. I was ready to kill him for the information."

"But you didn't."

"No, he ran outside. I caught up with him and forced him back into the apartment, but it was useless. He knew nothing."

"Was the girl gone when you came back with Finchley?"

"Yes, she was gone. That was the last I saw of her?"

"You didn't look for her?"

"There was no time. When the police arrived we decided not to mention the girl at all."

"What about the concertina?"

"It was gone, with the girl."

Jerry sucked at his cigarette, looked at Rodriguez. The fat man went to the window, moved the curtains a fraction of an inch, and peered out.

"Still there," he announced. He

looked at Jerry. "Are you satisfied with what he knows?"

"I guess so."

De Ordas looked defiant. "Now let me propose a deal," he said. "We can help each other. I'll split the money with you."

"Do *you* know where it is now?" Jerry asked.

"Finchley knows."

Jerry shook his head. "No, he doesn't. I've just seen him, and he's still looking. I don't need you for that."

De Ordas sagged back, defeated. "Well, at least — " He looked at the windows again. His face was gaunted with revived fear. "At least you will keep your promise?"

"I promised you a chance," Rodriguez said. "You shall have it."

He opened the door and said: "Carlos. Your gun."

The little man in the brown hat was there, the gaps in his teeth showing as he grinned. He obeyed without question, reached in his back pocket and handed a heavy Colt .45 to Rodriguez.

De Ordas stood up, his face suddenly haggard. Rodriguez handed him the blue gun, butt first.

"Here is your chance."

"I do not understand."

"You will leave here. Now."

"But — "

Rodriguez shrugged. "Take it or not, as you choose."

De Ordas' long face worked as he reached for the heavy gun. He stared at it, holding it in the flat of his palm.

"They will kill me if I go out now," he whispered.

"You have a chance," Rodriguez repeated. "More than you would give any of us."

De Ordas straightened, regarded them with a dawning, crooked smile. He flipped the gun around and pointed it at Rodriguez.

Jerry exploded: "Of all the fool things — !"

De Ordas was contemptuous, his face

changing from fear to cold, malignant fury.

"I made an error in coming here," he said softly. "I should have known that at once. Do not move, please."

Rodriguez was scornful. "Say your piece, pig."

"I was mistaken to think you were men of conscience. You understand nothing. I offered you a fortune, power. You laughed at me, even tried to frighten me."

"Tried?" Rodriguez grinned.

De Ordas said: "With this gun, I've nothing to fear. You've given me a better chance than you suspected. You will help me now, by coming with me."

Rodriguez said: "In exchange for your own safety, you'd offer me to your hired gunmen?"

"Exactly."

Rodriguez said: "Well, go ahead." He started for the door. De Ordas pointed the big Colt at the little fat man.

Rodriguez walked on. His hand was on the doorknob when Ordas pulled the trigger.

There was just a futile click. Jerry, halfway across the room in a swift lunge, pulled up, feeling foolish. Rodriguez turned towards de Ordas with a little chuckle, exhibited his hand. He had the magazine to the automatic in his palm.

"I was curious to see," he said, "if a hyena can change his color. Apparently not."

De Ordas stared down at the gun in his hand.

"It was empty," he whispered.

"Assuredly. And now — you will leave. I am a hospitable man, but you try my patience," Rodriguez said bitterly.

Carlos grinned and held the door open. De Ordas moved like a blind man toward the corridor.

Rodriguez said: "See that he gets safely to the street, Carlos." He turned to Jerry. "Unless he is no longer useful to you?"

"I don't think you ought to — "
Jerry began.

"This does not concern you, *amigo*.
He would have killed me."

"But those men out there . . . "

"His friends. The *Seguridad*. They
will take care of him. There is
nothing you can do, Jerry. Remain
here, please."

Jerry pulled up the window shade
and stared down at the windy street.
He felt a little sick. He stood with
his shoulders hunched, watching the
sidewalk. In a moment de Ordas
appeared, directly under him outside
the entrance of the café. No one else
came out with him. He looked up and
down the street, then started to walk
swiftly toward Sixth Avenue. He was
almost running. He was halfway up
the block when two shadows detached
themselves from a nearby doorway and
trotted methodically after him . . .

17

THE street seemed strangely quiet when Jerry left the café. The wind nipped at his heels; the yellow afterglow was gone from the sky. It was hard to realize that he had just witnessed a skirmish in an underground war that was going on all over the world, a war fought by the homeless and desperate against the forces that had scattered them over the face of the earth. He shivered a little and crossed the empty lanes of Washington Square. It was growing colder. Overhead, the moon rode as a clear white crescent above the geometric outlines of the buildings. Jerry felt vaguely forlorn, farther from a solution to Hamilton's death than ever before. He wondered what it was like to be dead and forever cold, like the moon up there or like little Mr. Gantredi.

A red cab was parked a few doors up the street, its motor throbbing softly. Jerry turned toward it. The driver was a dim shape behind the wheel, saying: "I'm occupied, mister."

The man who reclined with crossed legs in the back seat said easily: "It's all right. Get in, Jerry."

It was Bakerman. He looked tired and gray in the dim interior of the cab.

"You bloodhound," Jerry said. "I'll find my own cab."

Bakerman said: "We might as well share this one, Jerry. Wherever you go, I go."

"How did you find me down here?"

"I never left you." The gray-haired man grinned. "I've been tailing you since you left the Globe building."

Jerry stood still. "Then you saw de Ordas?"

Bakerman sat up straighter. "Jerry, you touch off fireworks wherever you go. I'm not quitting you now."

Jerry felt annoyed.

"Where I'm going now, they don't like cops. You'll queer my play."

"What play is that?" Bakerman asked casually. "Where are you going?"

Jerry leered.

"To bed," he said. "And maybe with a blonde."

He slammed the cab door shut and strode off down the street. A yellow taxi slid around the corner and he tumbled inside.

"Step on it, driver. Police business."

The cab lurched around the first corner and screamed north up Third Avenue. Jerry struggled up on the back seat and peered through the rear window. Bakerman's cab was close behind.

"Ten bucks if you can shake that guy," Jerry said.

"I'll try," said the driver. He didn't sound very optimistic. After a moment he added: "Where do you want to go, anyway?"

"The Nugget Club," Jerry said. "That's in Brooklyn."

266

Sighing, he looped his wrist through the door strap and gloomily surveyed the streets. Evidently the cabbie was making the most out of a good thing, going to Brooklyn by way of the Midtown Tunnel and via Queens. Jerry leaned forward.

"I'd like to get there, chum, by eight. Tonight, that is."

"You want to shake that guy first, don't you?"

Jerry looked over his shoulder. A red cab with a yellow hood was half a block behind them.

"Forget it," he said. "Let's dig for nuggets."

If he could find Stephanie, he reflected, he would have the key to unlock all the puzzles in the case. Somehow, the money that motivated the others in the case didn't seem important now. Any number of people might have killed Frank Hamilton, since his enemies reached far back into the past. But he had to find Steve first. The initials *J.L.* in her address book might stand for Johnny Lisbon, and that would tie into Patti Duggan's note implying that she knew something about Stephanie. The idea intrigued him.

The cab stopped for a red light and Jerry looked back again. He was astounded to see no pursuing hack in sight.

"Stop at the nearest telephone," he told the driver.

At a corner drugstore, Jerry took the number he had copied from Steve's telephone book and dropped a dime in the slot to dial AL2-2250. There was a long wait, and he had just decided that the number meant nothing at all connected with the case when the telephone clicked and a man's blurred voice said:

"Yeah?"

"Johnny?"

"Johnny who?"

"Johnny Lisbon," Jerry said. "Is he there?"

The man said: "You a wise guy?"

From beyond his voice came a thumping sound and a shrill woman demanding, "Who is it, Pa?" Then the man's voice again, still blurred and faint, said: "Some guy askin' for Johnny."

Jerry said: "Well is he there?"

The telephone was silent for a moment. Then the man said: "You know damn well he ain't here."

"Well, where is he?" Jerry asked.

"He's dead, you son of a bitch."

The telephone clicked sharply. Jerry felt dull surprise that Steve had actually had Lisbon's home number. It didn't make much sense.

There was a pawn shop next to the drugstore, and a sign in bright, winking orange, announced that Uncle Joe's was open all night. The windows glittered. Jerry paused as his eye fell on an object among the cluttered display of unredeemed articles.

It was a small, red, badly battered concertina.

He stood still, turning an idea over in his mind. Then, waving to his driver to wait, he went into the pawn shop. Three minutes later he came out as the possessor of a small, wailing, reedy set of bellows and sank back in his cab seat.

Two blocks behind them, a red cab with a yellow hood also slid into motion, following them.

★ ★ ★

At a quarter to eight the Nugget Club was just warming up for the dinner crowd. The building was a long, three-storied affair in the shape of an el that angled around the corner. Jerry stood on the sidewalk, listening to distorted snatches of music from a seven-piece orchestra. Colored lights streamed from the dance floor windows and the bar. Jerry shivered in the wind and trudged across the parking lot to the back entrance.

The concertina under his arm made a thin wailing sound as he pushed open the stage door.

The music was loud, brassy. It poured in a torrent down the narrow, dingy corridor, beating against him in waves of floor-thumping rhythm. A bald man in a dirty white shirt and flannel trousers brought his chair down from its angle against the wall and looked up.

"What do you want, bub?" he bellowed.

Jerry fastened the concertina bellows shut. He waved his arms. The music from the dance floor came to an abrupt stop. The silence was deafening.

"I'm looking for — " Jerry shouted, then lowered his voice. "I want to see Patti Duggan."

The doorman scratched gingerly at his scalp.

"You Jerry Benedict?" he asked.

"Uh-huh."

"You'll find Patti's room around the corner in the hall. First door to your left."

"Thanks, bub," Jerry said.

The door had a red paper star tacked to its central panel. Jerry paused, listening to a muted murmur of voices and the clink of glasses from the bar, then he tucked the concertina under his arm and walked into Patti Duggan's dressing room.

A man said admiringly:

"Ain't he prompt!"

A battered tin alarm clock on the dressing table read exactly eight. The room was small, windowless, with paint peeling from bare plaster walls. A poster on the inner panel of the door had a lush and revealing posture of Patti Duggan, the thrush of the Nugget Club, Dancing Nightly, $2.00 minimum.

Patti Duggan, in the flesh, wasn't there.

In her place were two unpleasant-looking men. The one who had admired Jerry's promptness was a burly giant with four gold teeth that glistened with his grin. His checked suit would have looked good on a horse — and on second thought, Jerry decided, it looked good on him, too. His companion was a dark, swarthy minor edition of the big man, perhaps five years older, and sporting a green bow-tie. Both of them inspected Jerry with a calm meticulous interest.

A bottle of gin, half empty, stood on the dressing table.

"Excuse me," Jerry said, "I was looking for Patti Duggan."

He started to back out, wondering if he could make it. He didn't. The man with the gold teeth said:

"This is Patti's room, mister."

A flicker of worry needled through Jerry's mind. He paused with his hand on the doorknob. The little man said: "Patti ain't here. What you want to see her about?"

"She knows," said Jerry. "She sent for me. I hope nothing's happened to her." He wasn't too optimistic, because anything was likely to happen with four hundred thousand dollars floating around in loose cash.

The little man said: "Nothing's happened to her. She just ain't here. We'll take you to her." He jerked his head toward the larger edition of himself. "This here's Joaquin. I'm Felipe." He poured himself a stiff jolt of gin, let it gurgle down his thin throat, and brought his head back to level to stare at Jerry. "The last name is Lisbon, mister. Johnny Lisbon was our brother."

Joaquin, the big one, rumbled: "Have a drink, chum."

Jerry decided he might as well be friendly. The gin was white lightning that burned down his throat and bounced in his stomach. He shuddered, closed his eyes, and let Joaquin pour another. Both men had sleek black hair that smelled of pomade. The big man's gold teeth glittered as Jerry adjusted the concertina under his arm.

"Patti said you were an all-right Joe," Joaquin rumbled. "But she's a scared chick, so we said we'd take you to her."

"And where is that?" Jerry asked.

"Out to our house. Out to Ma's."

"Where Johnny lived?"

"That's right," said the big man. "Where Johnny lived, until that son of a bitch knocked him off."

"You mean Frankie?" Jerry asked.

"Who else?" Joaquin rumbled. He wiped his mouth with the back of his huge hand, corked the gin bottle, pocketed it, and looked at Jerry. "You come alone?"

"I hope so. There was some fuzz tailing me, but I think I got rid of him."

"Goddammit, ain't you sure?"

"Maybe I'd better look around," Jerry suggested.

The Lisbon brothers looked dubious, then Felipe waved a generous hand. "Sure, go ahead. You ain't runnin' away. We want you should trust us, pal. Go see if the copper's in the joint."

The thumping rhythm of the orchestra made the floor shake as Jerry stepped into the hall. The dance floor of the Nugget Club was napkin-sized, crowded with couples who merely swayed in a form of ritualistic enchantment. Diffused purple spotlights made the dance floor hazy. Beyond a heavily draped archway was a halfmoon bar with customers perched on tall, red leather stools. Jerry maneuvered his way past the percussions of the drummer, skirted the dance floor, and bumped hard into a blonde in a scarlet gown. Her escort scowled; the girl gave him a dazzling smile. Her dress was much too tight in all the right places.

There was no sign of Bakerman in the bar. Returning to the dance floor, he paused as the blonde he had bumped into slid past and said: "Hi, Red." The man with her gave Jerry a furious look and pulled her roughly away.

Diagonally across the floor was the street entrance, and two men came in as Jerry sought out the Lisbon brothers. The newcomers wore Ivy League overcoats of dark blue, with narrow lapels. They didn't bother to take off their hats. The shorter one, with a thin straw-colored moustache, saw Jerry, said something to his companion, and started toward him. The blonde and her escort swayed between them for a moment, her eyes measuring Jerry speculatively. He started for the door leading back to the Lisbon brothers — and was halted by the man with the sandy moustache.

"Going somewhere, Mr. Benedict?"

He didn't like the young man's pale stare, nor the way they both kept their hats on and their hands in their pockets.

"Perhaps not," Jerry said.

"Better make up your mind to it. You're going somewhere — with us," said the moustached young man. From behind him came the moan of a saxophone as one of the orchestra took a solo. In a voice that was little more than a whisper, the young man said: "George Chalett wants to see you."

Jerry said: "George? Well, I don't want to see him. Not just now."

"Yes, you do. Last time was just a

warning, you see." The blond boy spoke as if he had a college education. "You had a little accident with your cab, remember? That was just a warning, to make you behave, old man."

"What does George want to see me for?" Jerry asked.

The blond boy was getting a little nervous.

"Just come along and find out."

The Lisbon brothers were still mysteriously absent. Jerry felt his hand go sweaty. Baby spotlights swept over the crowded floor, and from the press of dancers a girl's yellow hair glistened and red lips smiled at him.

"Don't you like me, Red?" asked the blonde girl.

"I'm crazy about you," Jerry said. He turned to the boyish gunman and said, "Pardon, old chap. I have a dance with the lady." He tapped the girl's escort on the shoulder. The man scowled as she slipped readily into Jerry's arms. She smelled nice, but her body was too warm under his hands as he started to guide her into the throng of dancers. Chalett's young messenger scowled, looked undecided; but the girl's escort was one who knew his own mind. His hand was rough on Jerry's shoulder, swinging him out of the girl's arms.

"Pick on somebody else, you bastard, or I'll — "

Jerry swung a hard left. His fist connected squarely with the man's jaw, knocked him head over heels into Chalett's two men. There came a splintering of wood as the three men went down among the ringside tables. Someone screamed. From the corner of his eye Jerry saw the two Lisbon brothers finally burst onto the floor. Chalett's blond boy got to his feet first. He had a pistol in his grip, and his pale eyes were venomous.

"That's the payoff, sucker — !" he said.

The blonde in Jerry's arms turned

into a frantic snake, trying to get out of the way. He shoved her hard into the milling dancers and ducked sidewise in the other direction. A gun boomed hollowly and a woman began screaming at the top of her lungs. The rhythm of the orchestra melted into a wailing dissonance as the musicians stampeded for safety.

The blond boy was standing on a chair, looking for Jerry. He started to raise the pistol again, and there came another hard, rapping report. The boy stood on tiptoe on his chair dropped his gun and did a swan dive to the floor. His companions vaulted under a table.

Someone shoved Jerry hard in the back.

"Get going!"

Chalett's hood struggled dazedly to his feet, his left arm limping. He still clutched his gun. Blood smeared his overcoat.

"Hit the back door," Jerry gasped to the man behind him.

The corridor behind the orchestra dais was jammed with excited musicians. Jerry plowed through them to Patti Duggan's dressing room, but it was empty. The shrieks of panicked dancers came from behind them as every one tried to get out at once.

Jerry turned to the man who had shoved him. It was Bakerman. The gray-haired detective had a big Colt in his hand, the muzzle still leaking pale smoke.

"My God, and I wanted to get rid of you!" Jerry exclaimed.

"Good thing you didn't. I had to wing that hophead, or he'd have nailed you for sure." Bakerman surveyed the corridor. "Let's get out of this."

They hit the back door simultaneously, burst into the sudden coolness of the night. The parking lot behind the Nugget Club was alive with shadows. Two of the shadows detached themselves from the nearby wall and became the Lisbon brothers — Felipe, the small one, and Joaquin, the giant.

They looked annoyed.

"You and your funny business," said Felipe. He cocked his head and listened to the uproar from inside the club. Then he turned to stare at Bakerman. The detective had pocketed his gun and his face was blank. Felipe said: "Who is this guy?"

"Some drunk," said Jerry quickly. He waved an arm at Bakerman. "Beat it, toad. Stop hanging around."

"Some people," said Bakerman, "have no sense of gratitude."

He started off at a wavering gait toward a red cab parked by the sidewalk. The Lisbon brothers watched him go with suspicion. From somewhere came the faint keening of a siren.

Felipe said: "Well, let's get out of here."

They pounded across the parking lot, scaled a low wooden fence, and raced up a narrow alley cluttered with ash cans. On the next street a car was parked, motor idling. The Lisbon brothers seemed to know what they were doing. Big Joaquin shoved Jerry into the rear seat, piled in after him, and fell back with a lurch as Felipe gunned the gas pedal and they roared off.

They had gone six blocks before Felipe spoke again.

"What happened back there?"

Jerry looked at the back of the little man's head.

"Some gunsels had an invitation for me, from George Chalett. They wanted me to come along with them."

Felipe made a whistling sound. "And you fogged 'em?"

Jerry thought of Bakerman, but decided it would be best to keep the detective out of it. He said:

"Well, it wasn't a little Indian that did it." He looked curiously at the dark streets flickering by. "Where are we going?"

"Why, to Ma's," said Felipe. "That's where Patti's staying, and she wants to see you, doesn't she?" Felipe took one hand from the wheel and pulled the bottle of gin from his topcoat pocket, passed it back to the rear seat, where Joaquin took it.

"Let's have another drink," said the little man.

18

THE house was on the outskirts of the city, toward Canarsie, and stood detached from its neighbors on a corner lot facing the salt marshes bordering the sea. The wind blew steadily here, and felt warmer, smelling of the Atlantic and the salt creeks. Felipe Lisbon ran the car expertly up a side driveway and got out, slamming the door. Joaquin nudged Jerry to the sidewalk ahead of him.

"Ma's been waiting for us," said little Felipe.

Lights shone dimly from behind the frowsily curtained windows. The front lawn was a desolation of barren weeds framed in a sagging picket fence. Jerry kicked an empty can noisily as he went up the brick walk to the porch. There was Victorian scroll-work on the veranda roof, two or three broken-down rockers, and a wooden glider hanging from rusty chains hooked to the porch ceiling. The street beyond was dark and lonely, and Jerry wondered where Bakerman had gone. The next moment he was inside, pushed uncompromisingly by the flat of Joaquin's big hand.

A woman's voice screamed shrilly:

"That you, boys?"

"It's us, Ma!" Felipe answered. "We got him!"

The hallway smelled of stale cooking, dust, and moldy drapery. A door slammed somewhere beyond the dark walnut staircase, then sliding doors were shoved violently aside to the right to reveal a dim, overstuffed parlor. A little gray-haired woman in a gingham flowered dress stood there, arms akimbo, staring at them through steel-rimmed spectacles.

"Your pa's drunk," she announced. Evidently this was the mother of the Lisbon *frères*. She did not exactly remind him of Whistler's Mother, particularly with the open bottle of beer in her hand. Her mouth was like a trap as she examined Jerry, nodding approvingly, and brushed wispy hair from her forehead. "Take 'em upstairs," she said. "Patti's raisin' hell up there."

Felipe turned to Jerry with a grin. "Up you go, pal."

Ma said: "You have any trouble with him?"

Joaquin rumbled out a belly-laugh.

"He thinks Patti sent us for him, Ma."

The little woman snorted, looked at Jerry with disgust, and said: "What a goddam dope."

Felipe gestured to the stairs again. "Up you go."

Jerry hesitated. "Is Patti up there?"

"She sure in hell is."

He had a feeling that all was not as it should be as he mounted the dark staircase. The house vibrated gently in the steady pressure of the wind that blew from the open sea. The little gray-haired woman scurried on ahead, down the barren hall to a white-painted door in the rear of the second floor. To Jerry's left, another open door gave him a glimpse of a bedroom. A short, fat man was sprawled on the bed, an empty bottle in his hand. His snores were heavy and uneven. Felipe nudged Jerry on, said: "Pa's never been the same since John got his."

Joaquin rumbled: "He usta be able to hold his liquor."

The gray-haired little woman paused at the other door in the hall and fished for a key in the capacious pockets of her gingham dress. She pulled out a soiled handkerchief, a bottle opener, a small .28 nickel-plated revolver, and finally a key ring, from which she selected one for the lock.

"This usta been John's room," Felipe volunteered.

Jerry went in. The moment he saw Patti Duggan, he knew his misgivings had a firm foundation. The girl's lemon-colored hair was disheveled, and there was an ugly blue bruise on the side of her little jaw. Her face was white and frightened as they all trooped inside, and she huddled back behind the bed, hands splayed flat against the wall. Her dark eyes flickered to Jerry.

"You fool," she whispered. "What did you come here for?"

"Shut up," said Ma, "or I'll bat you one again."

Jerry said: "You wanted to see me, didn't you?"

"But not here," Patti said. "God, not here. They're all crazy, can't you see?"

Felipe said: "You shut up, Patti. Don't talk like that. You listen to Ma and shut up."

The girl's dress had been torn down one side. Her wan little face twisted with a spasm of fear.

"It's about Johnny," she said. "I wanted to stay out of it, but they're crazy, they think it's a personal feud, or something, and they're after Johnny's killer. They think just because I was his girl I'm part of the family now, and they're making me go in with them. Honest, Mr. Benedict, they made me get you down here because they figure you know who killed John. I told them you didn't know, but they wouldn't pay attention. They're all blood-crazy, Mr. Benedict."

Ma said placidly: "Now, Patti, we talked about this before, and you said you'd help us. God help you, if you don't." She sat down in a Boston rocker. "I wish to Christ Pa hadn't finished that bottle."

"I got some gin, Ma," said Joaquin.

There was a moment's respite while the gin was passed out, and Jerry examined his surroundings, curious about this room that had been John Lisbon's. Evidently Johnny had made several gestures toward providing his family with sumptuous furniture and then given up in despair. The blinds, drawn all the way down, were tattered and frayed along the edges. There was a dark, scarred walnut wardrobe, a closet, and modern dresser barren of everything except a heavy, silver-framed portrait photo. The expensive frame looked out of place in these squalid surroundings, but it was not that which caused Jerry to suck in his breath and freeze where he stood, staring at the photo.

It was like a blow between the eyes. The portrait was that of a girl, and the girl was Stephanie Farley.

There was no mistake, although her dark hair was arranged in a sophisticated upsweep that made her oval face look fresh and piquant. It was like a revelation of all that Stephanie could be, he thought dizzily, this portrait transforming what had been a rather attractive girl into a beautiful, completely feminine creature. He didn't know it at the moment — there were too many other thoughts whirling in his mind — but he fell in love hopelessly and forever with Steve Farley, as he stared at her portrait then.

Dimly, he heard Ma Lisbon's chuckle.

"Twisted your guts a bit, didn't it?"

He turned to her, his face white and strained.

"How did that picture get here?" he asked.

"Wish we knew," said Ma. She rocked back and forth in her chair. "John brought it home one night, that's all. He didn't often sleep here, I can tell you that — had a big apartment on Park Avenue, he did. He never told us who she was, or how he got it. But that's why he was killed, all right; that's why my oldest boy was murdered."

Jerry was incredulous. "Because of this picture?"

"Over what he planned to do with it," said the woman.

"And what did he plan to do with it?"

Felipe took a hand. "We ain't sure, pal. But he knew something about that dame, and he kept talking about getting a lot of money for what he knew. Kept bragging how he had Frank Hamilton by the tail, and how Frank was going

292

to pay off plenty."

"But what did he know?" Jerry insisted.

Felipe shrugged. "That's why you're here, pal. You tell us."

"I don't know anything about her," Jerry said. "Certainly nothing to blackmail Hamilton with."

"No? Johnny found out somethin' which nobody else knew — and you bein' her fellow, we figure you know it, too."

"You're wrong," Jerry said earnestly. "I wish I knew, but I don't even know where she is, though I've been trying hard enough to find her."

Patti whispered from her corner:

"See? I told you he was crazy about her. He'd help you find her, if he could."

Ma Lisbon stopped rocking in her chair. Her sharp little face betrayed violence under the wrinkles of her age.

"Is that right?" she rasped. "You in love with that girl?"

"That's right," Jerry nodded.

"And you don't know where in hell she is?"

"Would I be here if I did?" Jerry asked. "Patti sent me a note saying she could help me find her. That's why I came. Would I stick my neck out at the Nugget Club, otherwise? I'm just as anxious to find out who killed John as you are, but knocking me around for information isn't going to help, because I haven't any yet, that's all. Patti doesn't know anything, either. But here's something to think about: if John was shaking down Hamilton because he knew something about the girl, it's a cinch that Frankie had him knocked off. But that isn't going to help you, either, because Frankie was killed last night."

Felipe made a spitting sound. "Hell, we know that."

Jerry whirled around to him.

"But do you know who did it?" he rasped.

"We figure maybe it was the dame,"

Felipe said. "John knew something about her, he brought her picture home a week before he disappeared, and then he had this fight with Hamilton and he came back here pretty badly mugged up. Next night he said he was going to fix Frankie good, said something about getting him through the girl, and he went out and we never seen him again. We figure he went to the girl and she crossed him up somehow and tipped Frankie off so Frankie could get him in the back. Nobody could beat John to the draw, I'm telling you that for a fact, and if he was dumped in the river it's because that dame doublecrossed him somehow."

"That's crazy," Jerry said, but he did not sound convincing. He remembered the telephone number in Stephanie's book, and he knew that the number was to the phone in this house. "Talk won't get us anywhere, anyway. You smacked Patti around and got me down here. Now tell me why."

There was silence for a moment in

the little room. Joaquin looked confused and stared at his smaller, older brother. Felipe chewed his lip worriedly. Ma Lisbon finished the bottle of gin and stood up. She was the only one who seemed decisive.

"Somebody's goin' to pay for my boy's death," she said.

"Frankie's already paid," Jerry said. "He's dead."

"But that girl ain't."

"She had nothing to do with it," Jerry said. His hands were sweating. "I'll stake my life on it."

"Pretty sure, ain't you?"

"I'm sure, yes."

"Well, suppose you take us to her and let us decide about that," said the little woman.

"But I don't know where she is," Jerry said.

"Maybe you got an idea where to find her?"

"No, I don't."

Joaquin said: "I'll knock it out of him, Ma."

"You shut the hell up," said the little woman. "All you know what to do is use your hands." Her eyes regarded Jerry shrewdly. "You're a nice-lookin' young feller, and Patti says you're all right. Maybe you are and maybe you ain't, but I think you're tellin' the truth."

Felipe offered: "He plugged one of Chalett's boys in the Nugget Club, Ma, so he's got guts enough, anyway."

The little woman whirled, her face going sharp.

"What's Chalett got to do with this?"

Felipe joined Joaquin in looking confused. He licked his lips fearfully for a moment.

"I forgot to tell you, Ma. He was mixed up in that thing on Waverly Walk, too. He was there. It was in the papers, but I forgot to read that part of it to you."

Ma Lisbon's eyes filled with bitter dismay.

"You forgot?" she shrilled. "You *forgot?*"

Felipe said hastily: "Now wait a minute, Ma — "

He lifted an arm as if to ward off a blow as the little woman advanced toward him. Patti Duggan sucked in her breath and huddled deeper in her corner. Big Joaquin made an uneasy rumbling sound in his throat. But as suddenly as it had come, Ma Lisbon's fury abated and turned to deep, despairing bitterness.

"That's what it comes to, havin' to depend on you two bastards. Just because I can't read, I got to depend on you. Maybe John went bad lookin' for easy money, but at least he was smart, he had brains, and I could depend on him. But you — pah!"

Felipe discreetly said nothing. His swarthy face was shining with sweat as the little woman turned away toward Jerry. Jerry tucked the concertina more securely under his arm — he had never for a moment let it go — and met her gaze with level eyes.

"Is that right?" she asked. "Is Chalett

mixed up in this, too?"

"I don't think — " he began.

"Shut up," she said. "I'm beginnin' to see a way out for you, boy. You're lucky. If I let Joaquin loose on you, you'd have more than a headache tomorrow, I can tell you." She sat down in her rocker again. "The thing to do is ask Chalett."

"Ask him what?" Felipe inquired.

"Where the girl is, you goddamn dope!"

Joaquin rumbled eagerly: "Yeah, that's it. Let's ask Chalett. I'd like to see that son of a bitch."

Jerry said: "Wait a minute. He's tough. And he's after me right now — "

Ma Lisbon made a snorting sound.

"My boys will take care of you. Besides, you'll be goin' to see him, instead of him pickin' you up. That'll make it different. That'll be the way you want it."

Jerry felt no enthusiasm for the idea.

"I don't like it," he said.

"Nobody asked you," said Ma. She

looked at Patti Duggan and smiled suddenly. "I guess we was wrong, Patti. I didn't mean for you to be mad at us, or anything. But you can see we got to find out the truth about John, one way or the other."

The lemon-haired girl said nothing her thin face turning to Jerry imploringly.

"You'll let her go?" Jerry asked.

"Why, sure," said Ma. "Patti's like one of the fam'ly, anyway."

Felipe and Joaquin had their hats on.

"Let's go," said Felipe. "Let's find George Chalett."

Walking downstairs between the two Lisbon brothers, it seemed to Jerry that he would have faced a firing squad more cheerfully than going on a wilful hunt for George Chalett. They were at the front door when the little woman came running hastily after them. She had a woolen scarf in her hand which she put around big Joaquin's neck.

"You better wear this," she said. "You might catch cold."

19

FOUR hours and many drinks later, Jerry no longer considered the search for George Chalett with trepidation. There had been smoky cellars and discreet hotel suites, the back rooms of night clubs, and now this lovely terrace penthouse on the East River. It was all very sedate, with a lavish elegance that made losing at the wheels almost a pleasure. The bartender, a Hollywood version of the perfect gentleman's gentleman, wore an immaculate mess jacket and wing collar and worked silent magic behind the bleached mahogany bar. He handed Jerry a frosted julep and said: "I beg your pardon, but — can you play that thing?"

"What thing?" Jerry asked.

"The concertina, sir."

Jerry had grown so accustomed to

the box-like contraption tucked under his arm that he had almost forgotten it. He gave the bartender a sly wink.

"Send not to ask for whom this concertina plays," he said. "It does not play for thee. This is a very special biffer squox." He paused, shocked. "My God, did I say that?"

"Whatever it was, yes, sir, you said it."

"Then I'm drunk," Jerry decided. "And I haven't found George Chalett yet. You sure you haven't seen him, ol' pal?"

"No, sir. Not this evening, sir."

It was a very elegant gambling dive, if a terrace penthouse could be called a dive. Through the windows he could see the moon on the river and the bleak cliffs on the Jersey side. A string quartet across the room was plucking out little Mozart airs that blended with the sedate atmosphere. Mozart, Jerry reflected glumly, had claimed to hear melodies all around him, all the time, and he needed only to reach into the air to snatch them for his musical scores. Jerry wished he could snatch George Chalett out of the air that way, but the gambler seemed to have vanished utterly from his usual haunts.

Already he'd had several drinks too many, since starting off with the Lisbon boys in search of the sinister George. The air was heavy with cigar smoke, the smell of perfume and corsages. Most of the guests were in the next room, where the two roulette wheels worked overtime separating them from their money. He wondered where the Lisbon brothers had gone, then decided he didn't care and returned to the bartender.

"I like this place," he said. "Who'sh the host?"

"I am," said the bartender.

Jerry said: "Don't kid me, brother, just because I'm a little drunk." Then he looked behind the bar and saw that a smiling little man had replaced the perfect gentleman's gentleman.

"I understand you and your friends

have been inquiring about Mr. Chalett," the man said.

"'S most important to have words with him," Jerry nodded.

"We wouldn't want any difficulties," smiled the little man. "This is a private residence, and while Mr. Chalett has been an occasional guest, I would not welcome a disturbance."

"No disturbance at all," said Jerry. "Just a word."

"All right, then. Come this way," the man decided.

They went down a short corridor into a private picture gallery. The little man quietly closed the door and snapped on the lights. The muted plucking of the string quartet was abruptly cut off. A cubist Picasso faced Jerry, under subdued light, an experiment in geometrical designs, flanked by a Dali and a small Gauguin. Dangling from the ceiling was a strange assortment of wires, with what seemed to be fishtails and pothooks moving slowly in the breeze.

The little man said: "I am an ardent collector and enthusiast of modern art and sculpture."

"That's sculpture?" Jerry asked, pointing to the slowly swaying mass of wire and metal foils.

"Three dimensional," the little man nodded. "Completely in the round, so to speak; dynamic rather than static, expressing motion in actuality rather than a passive, plastic reproduction."

"Did you ever hear of Sylvestor Johnson?" Jerry said. "He paints omelets."

The little man smiled his approval. "A genuis," he said. "A truly free mind. Do you know him, too?"

"Hell, I've bought him his omelets," said Jerry. The concertina under his arm wailed, and brought him back to the business at hand. "I thought you were taking me to see George."

"Mr. Chalett is not here. I chose this method," said the small man, "of removing you from my other guests without attracting undue attention.

Your friends have already been shown out, and now I must ask you to leave as well, Mr. Benedict."

The little man wasn't smiling any more. From the door behind Jerry stepped two neat-looking young men in evening clothes, who flanked him in a smooth, well executed maneuver. Their hands were very firm and steady on his elbows.

"Show Mr. Benedict to the street," said the little man.

It was just bad luck, Jerry thought, as he was whisked swiftly and efficiently down in a small private elevator. He brushed his sleeves as the two young men escorted him to the street door, smiled, nodded, and took their departure. The wind along the dark, deserted street blew in chilling gusts that cut through his topcoat. He was still ruminating on his bad luck when he saw the taxi parked by the sidewalk down the street.

It was a red taxi, and it looked very similar to the one Bakerman had used in following him about this evening.

It seemed like an explanation to the mysterious absence of George Chalett from his usual haunts. Jerry strode angrily toward the idling cab, yanked open the door, and leaned inside.

"Look here, Harvey, how do you expect me to get anywhere — "

The words abruptly stuck in his throat. The man inside the cab wasn't Bakerman, after all.

It was George Chalett.

The gambler's gun was pointed squarely at Jerry's middle.

"I understand you've been looking for me." Chalett's voice was soft and friendly. "Please step inside."

"Well, I — "

"Come, Mr. Benedict. You've been very anxious to find me, and now — " he smiled faintly — "we shall have a little chat."

20

THE sun came up with red fury, touching the lonely sand beach and the restless sea with brightening light. The wind had blown through the night with steady pressure, shaking the house as if with a giant's hand. The sullen roar of the surf filled the air with monotonous sound.

From his seat in the solid oak chair, Jerry could glimpse through the cottage window a bright triangle of glittering dunes, patched with dry October weeds. It was bitterly cold. His ropes were expertly tied, so that he suffered little loss of circulation in hands and feet; but his stubbled face showed the effect of sleeplessness and the strain of waiting for his next bout with George Chalett.

He had a vague recollection of going through the Holland Tunnel, and this glimpse of the sea looked like the Jersey coast. He couldn't remember anything else of the trip out here. There was an aching throb in the back of his head, where one of Chalett's men had sapped him as he leaned into the taxi on the East Side. Judging it to be about six in the morning, he decided he was hungry. It didn't look as if he was going to be fed. The cottage had a deserted feeling. It was clearly a summer cottage, now abandoned for the season. He wasn't gagged, for the very good reason, he supposed, that there was no one around for miles to hear him if he yelled. Nor did he feel like yelling. His head ached too much.

An iron cot was shoved against the opposite wall, a small maple bureau, a maple armchair, and an open, empty closet completed the furnishings. The glass in the single window facing the sea was broken, and the wind swept through the gap in a steady rush that numbed his whole body.

He decided to yell, anyway.

"Hey! Anybody home?"

The effort made his head ache worse, and his voice had a weak quality that scared him.

"Can anybody hear me?" he shouted.

It seemed a little silly. The sound of an auto bouncing over the dunes interrupted the monotonous thunder of surf and blatting of the wind. Jerry strained forward in his ropes, but he couldn't see the car through the window. Doors slammed, footsteps sounded in the hallway, and George Chalett came in.

The Lisbon brothers were with him.

The gambler was wearing an English gray ulster, a soft crushed felt hat, and a silk tie of pearl gray. He paused in the doorway, peeling off gray gloves.

"Hello, Chauncey," Jerry said.

Felipe Lisbon said: "Button your lip, pal."

The smaller of the Lisbon brothers had red-rimmed eyes and a twitchy mouth. Big Joaquin merely hulked in the doorway and took to paring his fingernails. Jerry relaxed as much as he could in the ropes that bound him to the chair.

"My chums," he said bitterly.

Felipe said: "Well, you doublecrossed us, didn't you? You made us think Mr. Chalett knew where the dame was."

"Well, doesn't he?"

George Chalett tucked his gloves in his coat pocket.

"I haven't got the girl," he said. His mouth was mildly amused. "I convinced your two friends of that."

"You must be running short of help," Jerry said. "Where's the fair-haired boy you sent to the Nugget Club?"

"Bellevue," said Chalett briefly. "It was a forty-five put him there, and you didn't shoot him, either."

Felipe said: "He lied to us all around, Mr. Chalett. He even convinced Ma, and she takes a lot of convincing."

Chalett stood in front of Jerry, cold and polite.

"Bobbie was a good boy, and I'm

going to miss him. That makes two I owe you, Benedict."

"You shouldn't use college boys for gun work," Jerry said. "But you don't owe me a thing. I'm frozen half to death already."

Joaquin gave a rumbling laugh.

"You ain't tasted nothin' yet, pal."

Jerry said nothing. The sun was up above the rim of the sea now, and from the corner of his eye he could see the aching glitter of the surf. He watched George Chalett draw up a chair with the toe of a highly polished shoe.

"Where is the girl?" Chalett asked softly.

"I don't know."

"Yes, you do. I don't make many mistakes," said Chalett mildly, "but they are good ones when I do. Hamilton got away with a good cut of my cash, and I want it back."

"I don't have your money," said Jerry.

"But the girl does. She got away with it in the concertina."

"That's just a guess," Jerry said.

"And a good one. Find the girl, and I'll find the money. And you know where she is."

Felipe said: "Don't waste your breath on the bastard, Chalett. Let Joaquin play with him and he'll be glad to spill his guts."

"My pals," Jerry said again.

" — you," said Felipe.

Chalett regarded Jerry calmly. "I know you have been hiding the girl since last night, Benedict. You've been hiding her in your own apartment."

"*My* apartment?" Jerry asked. "On Waverly Walk?"

"Your old one," Chalett said patiently. "On Seventy-Ninth Street. I looked in on it, and her things were there."

Jerry was shocked. "Her things were in my rooms?"

"Her suitcase yes. The bathtub was still wet, too. If I had been a moment sooner, I'd have found her in."

Jerry felt as if he had stopped breathing.

"But she wasn't there, though?"

"No."

"And she didn't come back?"

"She didn't return," Chalett said quietly. "So I decided to look in on you again and ask you where she might be."

"Hell," Jerry protested. "I didn't know she was hiding out in my place!"

Out of the confusion created by the gambler's words came bitter self-recrimination. He *should* have known, he reflected. That's what Stephanie's message to Bernice had meant. 'Tell him to stay in his own back yard.' It should have been interpreted as a message to him that she had taken refuge in his own rooms. He cursed his own stupidity.

"Joaquin," said Chalett quietly.

The big, hulking man shoved away from the wall with a twitch of his meaty shoulders.

"Joaquin," said Chalett. "Ask him where the girl is."

Jerry said: "Now wait a minute — "

Joaquin rumbled: "Where's the dame, pal?"

"I don't know."

Joaquin hit him with a ham-like fist. Jerry went over backward in the chair and crashed sidewise, the chair half on top of him. He felt as if his arm had been twisted half from its socket by the fall. He tried to struggle from the ropes, and Joaquin picked him up, chair and all, as if he had been a child, and set him upright on four legs again. Felipe's eyes glistened; Joaquin put his knuckles to his mouth. Chalett looked cool and composed.

"Just a minute," said the gambler.

The only sound in the room was the muted rumble of the surf and Jerry's hoarse breathing.

"What was the idea of this concertina?" Chalett asked. He held up the one Jerry had bought in the pawn shop. "Is this the one the girl had?"

"To hell with you," Jerry said.

Chalett said thoughtfully: "There's certainly no money in this one. Yet I'm told you carried it around with you all last night. Where is the money that was in it?"

"I don't know. I didn't take it."

"You only make it more difficult for yourself," Chalett said. "I have no desire to inflict physical punishment on you. I have always been friendly with the press, and I see no reason why you and I should not be able to settle this amicably."

There was blood inside Jerry's mouth, where Joaquin had hit him. He spit it out on the floor, just missing the shining toe of Chalett's shoe.

"That your idea of a friendly chat?" he asked.

"You insist on being difficult," Chalett said.

Joaquin said: "Shall I bop him again, Mr. Chalett?"

Chalett didn't seem to hear. His eyes rested on Jerry.

"Where is the girl, Benedict?"

"I don't know."

"Where is the money, then?"

"I don't know that, either," said Jerry. "Why don't you take my word for it? I'm just as anxious to find her as you are."

Chalett said carefully: "Where money is involved, especially large sums, a man's integrity is apt to weaken. I am sure you and the girl are partners in your hijacking venture, and I am sure you know where she is. She hid from the police in your room, while you were in jail, and presumably remained hidden there during the day just passed. You have the concertina, so you must have contacted her some time yesterday. Can you blame me if I am inclined to ignore your pretense of ignorance?"

Jerry said: "It's not the money that bothers you. It's because I pulled a gun on you in front of Wanda, and made you look silly. You'll have to fix me so your pals won't get similar ideas of standing up to you. Otherwise you might suffer an epidemic of welching on debts owed to you. So what's the use of telling you anything? You'll give me a rubdown anyway."

Chalett turned his head sharply to Joaquin.

"All right," he said. "Exercise him."

Joaquin grinned and shambled toward Jerry's chair.

Jerry said: "At least you could untie me — "

The big man's hand smashed across his mouth, rocked him back in the chair, returned back-handed and knocked the chair over again. This time there came a splintering crash as the legs gave way. The broken chair reduced his tight bonds to a loose tangle of lines. Jerry wriggled desperately to free himself, and Joaquin kicked him in the stomach.

"Ask him," said Chalett quietly.

"I'm askin'," said Joaquin.

Jerry caught his breath, got one arm loose, and grabbed at the big man's foot as it came for his head. The big man stumbled, came down on top of him as Jerry yanked. He was too weak to take advantage of the opportunity, however, and staggered away from Joaquin as the latter rumbled in rage and climbed to his feet. Jerry lunged crazily for the trim figure of the gambler, seated on the couch. A gun bloomed in Chalett's hand.

"Stay right there!"

Joaquin wrenched at Jerry's shoulder and Jerry smashed blindly at the big man's angry face. He felt cartilage break under his knuckles. Joaquin reeled away, blood spurting from his smashed nose.

Chalett's voice was sharp, bitter.

"By God, I'll fog you for this!"

Jerry swayed in the center of the room, sucking air into straining lungs. The kick in the stomach had done him no good at all. He measured the four paces that separated him from the gambler, wondered if he could make it before Chalett fired . . .

319

"Goddammit," said a voice from the doorway. "Everybody put 'em up!"

It was Ma Lisbon. The little gray-haired woman had a huge old Colt's .48, a relic of frontier days, and it was pointed unerringly at George Chalett's stomach.

"Up!" she shrilled. "Get 'em up!"

Chalett's brows made little creases between his eyes, and he hesitated, then decided on the wiser course. He put the gun aside and raised his hands. Joaquin just stood and gaped, his bloody handkerchief at his nose. Felipe licked his lips.

"Why, Ma," he said. "Ma, what you doin' here?"

"You no good son of a bitch," screamed the little woman. "I ought to bat your ears off!"

"We ain't done nothin', Ma!" Felipe whined.

The little woman's face reflected bitter scorn. She was wearing a round, misshapen hat slapped over her helter-skelter hair and a bright green coat with

320

a mousy fur collar wrapped around her silent figure. She waggled the big gun at her sons.

"Get out," she said. "To think I borned two such dumb bastards! Get out!"

Joaquin rumbled: "But. Mr. Chalett said — "

"Since when you takin' orders from him?" Ma shrilled. Her face was dark with fury. "You ain't got the sense of a flea, neither of you, lettin' him talk you into beatin' up Mr. Benedict, here. Get out!" She looked at Jerry and flourished her huge Frontiersman. "You, too, boy. Your friend is outside."

Jerry picked up his hat from a corner of the room, found the concertina under the couch, and buttoned his coat. His chest ached, as if every rib had been split by Joaquin's heavy shoe. There was no sound in the cottage except a weary sigh from George Chalett as he stepped outside.

The sunlight was a blinding glare on the sand dunes. Someone grabbed

Jerry's arm and piloted him toward a police sedan that was parked behind the house.

It was Bakerman. Jerry blinked at the gray-haired detective and drew a deep, painful breath.

"My aching back," he said. "I never thought I'd be so glad to see you again." He climbed slowly into the sedan. "What did you tell Ma Lisbon, that put her on our side?"

"I lost you after you left the Lisbon house," Bakerman smiled faintly. "So I had words with Ma Lisbon and told her that Chalett was only using her boys for monkeys. I also convinced her that you didn't know where your girl is."

"How did you do that?"

"I told her that we — the police — knew where she was. And I *do* know."

Bakerman deftly backed the sedan away from the house and over a grassy dune. There was a dirt road that wandered over a rickety causeway to the mainland. Jerry was silent, then said:

"All right, where is she?"

"In your apartment," Bakerman replied.

"You mean, she was." Jerry felt disappointed. "Even George Chalett knew that."

"No, she's there now. She came back again."

"And she's all right?"

"Sure, she's all right," said Bakerman. "Which is more than I'll be when I get home. My wife will raise hell with me for being out all night."

Jerry sighed. "I guess I really ought to spend more time at home, too."

21

JERRY'S two-room apartment was on the third floor of a brownstone house in the East Seventies. No mail waited for him in his box. The smell of cabbage came from Mrs. O'Brien's in the first-floor rear as he followed Bakerman up the stairs. He was excited by the thought that in a moment he would see Stephanie again, pleased that she had come to him for sanctuary.

Bakerman frowned at the empty, third-floor hall.

"I left Pease on guard here," he exclaimed.

Jerry used his keys to get in. The apartment was clean and masculine, but mingled with the rich scent of pipe tobacco was that of an elusive perfume. A woman had certainly been in the place; but there was no woman here now. The living room was spotless and empty. So was the bedroom. A sound came from the kitchen, and Jerry beat Bakerman to the swinging door.

"Steve?" he began.

Pease was seated at the table, munching an apple. A glass of beer rested at his right hand. The little ferret-faced detective was critically surveying an improvised gallery of oil canvasses propped on table, chairs, and kitchen cabinet. Pease looked up at Jerry and said:

"Hi. These things are screwy, ain't they?"

Bakerman said sharply. "Where did these come from?"

Pease shrugged. "This is the way I found 'em. They yours, Benedict?"

Jerry nodded. "I do some painting, too. I had them stacked in a closet, though, last time I saw them."

Pease said: "Well, I guess the girl was admiring them. But they sure look screwy to me."

"Where is the girl?" Jerry asked sharply.

"Out shopping. I put McCarthy on her."

"Did she see you?" Bakerman asked.

"Not a chance, Harvey. After she left, I come in to call your wife, like you told me to. She's pretty sore, Harvey."

Bakerman scowled. "What about the concertina?"

"It ain't here. I looked all over, too."

"Did she take it with her?"

"Nope. I don't figure she even brought it here, now."

Bakerman said to Jerry: "We didn't want to alarm her, so we held off questioning until you could do it. She'll tell you things she might not tell us." His thin, gray face was worried. "I only hope Dulcey don't tie a can to our tails for this."

Pease finished his apple, drained the beer from his glass. "She stayed here until about nine, Harvey, then she shopped the neighborhood groceries, bought a bag full of stuff, and come back about forty minutes later. But she came right out again. McCarthy and me tailed her to a beauty shop on Broadway. That's where she is now, gettin' a permanent. Can you tie that?"

It was already after ten, and Jerry felt as if someone had thrown sand in his eyes. His body ached all over. He longed for a hot shower and some sleep, but evidently he wasn't going to get it.

"Which beauty shop?" he asked Pease.

"Pierre's. You can't miss it."

Bakerman gave Jerry a critical look.

"You ought to be in a hospital," he said.

"Let's go to the beauty parlor," Jerry said.

★ ★ ★

Pierre's was one of a row of stores occupying the street floor of a tall Broadway apartment house. A uniformed cop stepped from among the passersby in front of the beauty shop and spoke to

Bakerman, after looking at his watch.

"She's been in there half an hour, Harvey. I think I'd better get back on my beat."

"Well, let's go in and talk to her, then."

The proprietor, Pierre, was a small man with a penciled moustache and thin black hair. He said, in answer to Bakerman's quiet question: "In a moment, m'sieur. I shall go and see."

They waited in the anteroom. A matronly woman came out and gave the three men a querulous look before accepting her mink coat from a girl attendant. The girl attendant looked at Jerry's stubbled beard and began to say something, then thought better of it as the proprietor reappeared.

"A dark-haired girl, m'sieur, is not here."

"She must be here," Bakerman said. "She was seen coming in, and she didn't come out."

"You are calling me a liar?" asked Pierre.

"I will, in a minute," said Bakerman. He pushed into the inner sanctum of the beauty shop. Several women were under the white metal dryers. But just a glance at their legs convinced Jerry that Steve was not among them. Nor did any of the other patrons even remotely resemble her.

Jerry turned angrily to the proprietor.

"Where is she?" he demanded. "Did she run out when you spoke to her, or what?"

The proprietor turned purple. "I say to you I had no young lady of that description! I am not accustomed to this barbarous treatment!" He lapsed into sputtering French. "*Je vous dis merde, m'sieur!*"

Jerry said: "For two pins, I'd — "

Bakerman put a restraining hand on his arm.

"Let's look in the back. Come on."

They went through a door in the rear, followed reluctantly by Pease. The door opened into a short corridor that ended in another glass door. Pushing through this, they found themselves in the lobby of the apartment building. They all paused and stared. Bakerman swore softly.

"She walked right on through," he said, and turned to Pease: "You sure she didn't know we were on her trail?"

"Positive."

Bakerman said: "Well, it's nobody's fault. She's just too smart for us."

Jerry sank down in one of the big lobby chairs. He felt unutterably weary. It seemed to him that Steve was getting herself deeper and deeper into a morass of murder, with no way out. Disappointment filled him with bitterness, and a lethargy sapped his remaining strength.

Bakerman said gently:

"You'd better turn in, Jerry. Don't worry about the girl. Judging from what we learned about her, she can take care of herself better than you can."

★ ★ ★

It was past noon when Bakerman took his departure, leaving Jerry in his rooms to shower and sleep. The hot water soothed his battered body, and he tended carefully to the bruises on his ribs. There was no doubt about it, Steve had deliberately given Bakerman and Pease the slip. What was most curious was the absence of the concertina. Jerry spent an hour searching through his rooms for the instrument, which the girl had certainly taken from Waverly Walk; but there was no trace of it. He also searched for any message Stephanie might have left him. He wouldn't have found it if it weren't for his shirt buttons.

Every one of his collar buttons had been replaced. The topmost shirt held the message, folded into the pocket.

"*I have no lock picks, but I used a hairpin on your door. Why didn't you tell me you can paint? P.S. I can sew, too.*"

The note was signed, *Steve*. Jerry

grinned, plucked out the collar button, and dropped it in a waste basket. He smoked several cigarettes, his eyes thoughtful; then got up, rummaged in his coat pocket, and pulled out the sheaf of doodled cartoons he had drawn of the suspects in the case. Scattering them over the bed, he studied the brief pencil sketches for a long time. They were all there — Lucy Quarles, George Chalett, Polders, Apple, Finchley, Steve and de Ordas. He pushed them around tentatively with a stiff forefinger, rearranging them, pairing them off in experimental groups. After a while a startled look dawned in his eyes. He rearranged the caricatures again, and then again. He sat down at the desk, finally, and picked up the telephone to call McConaughy.

"Bakerman just told me," the fat man said, "that you got away from Chalett. I got on Dulcey's ear and poured it into him, asking for a dragnet for Chalett and the Lisbon boys. He's sore as hell at Bakerman, by the way."

Did Harvey check those scraps of microfilm?"

"Yeah, he did that," McConaughy sighed. "And I hate to admit it, but you were right again. There was enough to show they were records of Hamilton's financial deals in the stock market. I guess he kept them to protect himself. Incidentally, I got some financial information on that Finchley guy. He's over-borrowed almost two hundred grand on the strength of his deal with Hamilton, and the banks and loan companies are ready to sit down on him, but hard."

"Fine," said Jerry. "Any dope on Stephanie Farley?"

"They're still searching. Nothing yet."

"Well, forget it," Jerry said briskly. "There's one thing you can do for me, Luscious. Call up everybody involved — including de Ordas, if you can find him, and tell them all I have the concertina. Tell each one I'll make a private deal — but pretend to each one that he's the only one I'm willing to talk business with. I'll meet them at Waverly Walk tonight."

"Hell," said McConaughy. "That's corny. You're just sticking your neck out." he paused. "You don't really have the concertina, do you?"

"I've got one like it," Jerry said.

"So you're going to bait a trap with yourself?"

"Something like that."

"You want the cops in it?"

Jerry said: "As you like, boss."

He hung up. Sleep dragged at him irresistibly as he lay on his back and studied the ceiling as if the answers were written up there. He knew he should be on his feet, making further inquiries; but the bed held him as if chained.

After a while, he slept.

★ ★ ★

He awoke the instant the telephone rang. He was astonished to find his

334

room in darkness. It was already past six. The telephone kept ringing shrilly, disturbing the quiet peace of his shadowed apartment. He yawned and picked up the receiver, held it clumsily to his ear while he groped in the darkness for a cigarette.

A soft, whispering voice spoke to him.

"Jerry? Is that you, Jerry?"

He took a deep breath, swallowed, and was silent. The silence spun itself out in the darkened room, while the whispering voice in the receiver became urgent.

"Jerry? Is that you?"

"Hello, Steve," he said.

"Thank goodness. Are you all right?"

"I'm fine. And you?"

"I — I'm all right, darling. But I was so worried about you." She grew concerned. "Are you angry about something?"

"You ran out on me," he said.

"Oh, I had to, Jerry. I can't explain now, but I will later, and you will see

335

that I had no choice."

"Where are you now?" he asked bluntly.

"I — I can't tell you that," she said.

"Where is the concertina? And the money?"

"I have it hidden."

"Where?"

"I'm going to pick it up tonight. Oh, Jerry — "

He said harshly: "You've given me a bad time, Steve."

"I'm sorry, darling. But I'm all right now. Really, I'm all right." Her voice paused. The sound of muted traffic came through the darkened windows, and the reflected beams of auto headlights passed across the ceiling. From somewhere overhead came the muted thump of a radio. The girl's voice kept whispering to him from out of the dark. "Jerry, I've had to do all this alone because it concerns me, personally. I've felt responsible, in a way, for all these horrible deaths. I felt I had to satisfy myself that none of it was really my fault."

"I think I understand," he said quietly.

"Do you, Jerry?"

"But Johnny Lisbon would have been killed, no matter what he knew about you."

"You do know about that, then. That's why I've been so frightened. Frank told me over and over again not to trust anyone. I didn't know what it was about, then. I had no idea Frank was — like he was. The more I learned, the more frightened I became. Frank was afraid the others would try to reach him by threatening me, if they found out who I was. And since then I've been afraid they would think I have the money. I went to your place yesterday, hoping to find you, and I waited hours; but I noticed some men watching your house and got out as soon as I could, so as not to involve you in this mess."

"I'm in it up to my neck already,"

he said grimly. "Look here, Steve — I want that concertina and the money you found in it."

There was a pause, then: "All right. Whatever you say."

"I want to see you now," he said. "As soon as possible."

"Where?" she asked.

"At Waverly Walk. In an hour."

The girl said: "I'll be there, Jerry."

Jerry said: "Be careful, Steve."

"I'll be careful."

22

THERE was darkness all around her. Stephanie closed the door softly, then leaned back and listened. There was no sound, no reaction to the remote click she had made in closing the door. All she heard was the thudding of her heart and the distant murmur of the city outside the house. There was nothing to see in the darkness of the room, no more than if she had been blindfolded.

She had a small Colt's .32 in her purse which she had taken from Jerry's apartment. She hoped she wouldn't need it. But she made sure it was there before going on.

She took a cautious step to her left, feeling for an armchair. No sound, no movement came from the musty darkness. A silver bracelet on her wrist tinkled softly and she paused to take it off. She stowed it in her pocket book and took a tiny pencil flashlight, and after a moment's hesitation, she thumbed the little button. The faint beam was lost in the darkness, but she made out enough of the room to satisfy herself that she was alone in it.

This living room of the third-floor apartment of Number 16 Waverly Walk looked as it had two nights ago, scantily furnished, chilly and deserted. The narrow beam of her light touched on the drawn window blinds, the empty bookshelves, the couch and the fireplace that had been used by 'Mr. Julian Street.' She settled the light on the fireplace, with its dry pile of logs on the andirons behind the curved copper screen, then she turned to investigate the other rooms of the apartment.

They were all empty.

She felt a little more secure when she returned to the living room. Turning to the fireplace, she put down her purse and groped in the darkness to remove the screen. The logs behind it felt dry and brittle and dusty to her fumbling touch. From behind the logs her searching fingers touched the leather end of the concertina she had hidden there on the night of Gantredi's murder. She breathed a quick sigh of relief and stood up, holding the bellows in both hands.

The darkness flowed around her, silent, thick with shadows. The leather of the concertina felt warm and smooth under her cold fingertips.

Turning to the telephone, she put the concertina down beside it and dialed, counting the dial holes with her fingertips in the dark. For a moment the fear that lived in her almost caused her to halt. She felt her throat grow tight as she heard the distant ringing of that other phone.

The phone that would be answered by a murderer.

It seemed a long time before a voice said briefly:

"Hello?"

Stephanie waited for her heart to stop pounding.

"Hello?" the voice repeated.

"This is Stephanie Farley," she said quietly. She was surprised at the steadiness of her voice when she spoke. "I want to talk to you."

"What about?" asked the other voice, curtly.

"The concertina," Stephanie said. "I've had it, all along, as you must have suspected."

"I'm not interested," said the voice.

Stephanie frowned. "I know you don't want the money, although I have that, too, all of it. But I should think you'd want the concertina back."

"Why?"

Stephanie said: "Your name is painted on it."

"Nonsense!"

Stephanie said: "But it is. There was a leather cover on one end, and when I pulled it off, there was our name."

Silence spun spider webs of shock and fear on the other end of the line.

The voice went harsh.

"All right. What do you want of me?"

"An explanation," Stephanie said.

"Nonsense," said the voice again. "You must want something from me."

"Only the explanation. I must have it. It's important to me. I want to know who I really am," she said, "and that's why I'm willing to risk everything by telling you about this."

"You're a fool," said the voice.

"Perhaps I am," said Stephanie, "but I must see you and I must talk to you."

"Where are you now?" asked the other.

Stephanie hesitated. "I'm on the third floor of Number 16 Waverly Walk," she said. "I'll wait up here for you. You'd better come in from the Harvey Street entrance, though — there may be some people in the lobby downstairs."

"Does anyone know you're there?"

She hesitated again.

"No one," she said.

"All right," said the voice. "I'll be there."

"How soon?"

"Quite soon," said the other.

The telephone went dead. It seemed to Stephanie that there was a duality to the click, as if it echoed in her ears. Her hands were trembling again as she cradled the telephone. The apartment still seemed to be empty. She took the small .32 revolver from her purse, selected an armchair in the dark, and sat down to wait out the minutes.

★ ★ ★

There was a change in the apartment, a change in the quality of the darkness or in the tautly spinning silence that filled the dim room. Stephanie listened, straining for the sound of a whispering footfall; but she heard and saw nothing.

Yet she knew, somehow, that she was no longer alone.

Someone was in the apartment with her.

Not more than ten minutes had passed since she put down the telephone, although she wasn't sure, because the darkness had put a cloak around the passage of time. She listened, but there was no sound. She tried to see, but there was nothing to see.

She stood up suddenly, holding the gun in taut fingers.

"Is anybody there?" she whispered softly.

No answer came from the brooding darkness. She wished, suddenly, that Jerry Benedict were with her.

The sound of a footfall came from the hallway.

"Who is there?" she asked sharply.

Someone answered from out of the darkness.

"Whom did you expect?"

Stephanie whirled, sucking in her breath, and reached for her pocket light. From nearby came a quick thud on the invisible carpet. She turned instinctively toward the sound, gun in hand — and instantly realized she had been tricked. The man in the hallway came up behind her as she turned away from the dark, arched entrance.

Something hard and cold was pressed into her back.

"I've come for the concertina — and the money, Miss Farley."

She felt completely confused. The voice was not the one she had expected. Cold fingers slid over her wrist and detached the gun from her grip with an almost gentle pressure.

The man was just a darker shadow among the other shadows.

"You have been very foolish, Miss Farley."

"I — I merely wanted to make a bargain," she whispered.

"You didn't expect me, though."

"No, I . . . I didn't."

As if to satisfy her curiosity, the man snapped on one of the lamps. The room leaped into startled existence.

The man was Dr. John Polders.

His right hand was swathed in bandages, but the fingers were free, holding his gun. He wore a green gabardine topcoat and a low-crowned green hat. He would have looked collegiate except for the bitterness behind his smile.

"How did you know I was up here?" she whispered.

"I came a little early. Your friend, Mr. Benedict, invited us all to a little meeting downstairs — obviously a snare and a delusion. I was alone in the first-floor apartment, however, when you made your call. You didn't know that this telephone was an extension to the one downstairs. I listened in, and came right up."

The doctor glanced around the room, his weak eyes settling on the concertina she had left on the desk.

"The money is still there?" he asked softly.

Stephanie nodded mutely.

Polders said: "An unexpected windfall. Frank Hamilton owed me a lot for all the years I worked for him, back in the old days; but I never really expected to get all of the money."

"It's not yours," Stephanie said.

"It is now, my dear."

"Then did you — was it you who killed Mr. Gantredi?"

Polders smiled.

She added: "And Frank Hamilton?"

Polders stopped smiling.

"I'm sorry," he said. His voice grew tighter. "I wouldn't mind discussing it with you, but unfortunately, you've invited someone else up here, and there is not time to spare."

The gun in his hand jerked up a bit.

Stephanie said: "What are you going to do?"

"Isn't it obvious?" Dr. Polders was trembling a little. "I don't want to kill you, but I can't let you go now."

Looking at his oddly glittering eyes, she knew she was going to die, but she felt curiously unafraid.

"Go ahead," she said levelly. "You don't dare."

Without warning, the lights went out.

In the stifling darkness, Stephanie heard a quick oath, felt a sudden movement of air beside her. A gun roared and flamed, splitting the blackness. Something crashed violently into her side, knocking the breath out of her.

Out of the darkness came a high, shrill womanish scream.

Stephanie was surprised to find herself on her knees. She could see nothing, but she heard a series of thumping sounds, someone's whistling breath, and then, out of the corner of her eyes, glimpsed something white and shapeless bending over her.

The whiteness exploded into blinding light.

23

AT eight o'clock Jerry Benedict paid off his cab at the corner of Waverly Walk and stood on the sidewalk, the wind whipping his coat around his legs. The green neon sign over Ernie's bar still winked a steady invitation. Swinging the concertina he had purchased in the pawn shop under one arm, he crossed the cobblestone street to the opposite pavement.

A shadow detached itself from the first house on Waverly Walk and called softly to him.

"Mr. Benedict! Please."

It was Wanda Dykes, wrapped in a cherry-red coat with a blue fox collar. Her face was wan in the dim light from the Colonial lamp. Her fear looked genuine this time.

"I'm so glad I caught you, before you went in."

"Are any of the others here yet?" he asked.

"Most of them." Her eyes touched the concertina he was carrying and grew wide. "Is that — is that the one that has all the money?"

"Let's go in and find out," he suggested.

"Oh, no, please! . . . Wait just a minute."

"What are you afraid of?"

"I'm sorry I ever got mixed up in this business. But please believe me — I'm in dreadful danger. If George Chalett — "

"Don't worry about him," Jerry said bluntly.

"But he'll kill me. He wants that four hundred thousand dollars, and he thinks I doublecrossed him!"

Jerry began walking down the cobblestone street, and the blonde kept pace with him, her high heels clicking rhythmically on the pavement. Within the sheltered dead end of Waverly Walk the wind was replaced by a chill

351

October calm. Overhead, the moon rode as a high, clear crescent in the glowing sky.

Wanda Dykes stopped him again at the entrance to Number 16.

"Please wait just a minute. You *must* help me!"

"The others are there already," Jerry said grimly. "What I have to say to you will have to be said to them, too."

Her face was pale in the gloom.

"Do you know who the murderer is, Jerry?"

"Yes, I do."

She seemed to stop breathing as they stood in the doorway.

"Will you tell me?" she whispered. "Now?"

"Yes, before you see the others. Please?"

She was standing very close to him, and he was taken by surprise again — though he shouldn't have been surprised at all — when her arms snaked around his neck and her red lips sought his. He jerked his head aside and pushed her roughly away.

"Oh, no, baby — you tried that one on me before!"

"But I — "

He stepped back to the curb, away from her, and something overhead caught his eye. For a moment he had seen a light in the windows above him; but it was gone when he carefully studied the façade of the old Georgian house. He started back to the lobby steps when he suddenly paused, struck by the significance of what he had seen. The light had been *on the third floor*!

Wanda Dykes came toward him again, her face contrite.

"Get out of my way," he said savagely.

He went down the three steps and burst into the lobby of Number 16. It looked much as it had on the first evening, with its red mohair bench, pastel walls, and ivory staircase to the upper floors. The door to the first-floor apartment was open. McConaughy was in the living room, apparently engaged in stalling off Lieutenant Dulcey's anger. Finchley sat like a worried little elf beside Wanda Dykes' secretary-maid, Apple. George Chalett leaned in grim solitude under the sunburst mirror. Jerry stood in the doorway and snapped abruptly:

"Who's up on the third floor?"

McConaughy looked relieved and happy to see him.

"Jerry! It's about time you showed up. I told Dulcey you'd be here, all right — "

"I don't care about Dulcey." Jerry ignored the startled faces that turned toward him. "Who else is in this house?"

"Nobody," said McConaughy. "Nobody at all."

"Did Stephanie Farley show up yet?"

Dulcey stepped forward, his blocky face grimly recalcitrant.

"Look here, Benedict, you seem to think I've nothing to do — "

Jerry ignored him. He said: "Keep

everybody down here, whatever you do. Just wait for me." He turned to cross the lobby. He was sure he had seen a light go off on the third floor, and there was no reason why anyone should be up there. He felt cold, his stomach queerly knotted, as he raced up the ivory staircase to the second floor.

Bakerman was standing in front of Mrs. Quarles' apartment door, his hand uplifted as if about to knock. The detective turned his gray head inquiringly, but showed no great surprise.

Jerry pointed to the door at the end of the hall.

"Did anyone come down from there just now, Harvey?"

Bakerman shook his head. "No, I haven't seen anybody. Where've you been?"

"Never mind. Have you got a gun?"

"Ever see me without one?" The tall detective pulled his Police Positive from his hip pocket. His tired face showed signs of interest. "What's up?"

"Let's go and see," Jerry said.

"But Dulcey asked me to get this dame — "

"It didn't do any harm last time you took my advice, did it?"

Bakerman grinned. "I guess it didn't, Jerry." He waggled his gun. "This time, let me go first."

The staircase door wasn't locked. The steps to the third floor were in darkness. Jerry's palms were cold and damp as Bakerman carefully eased open the door and was swallowed by the gloom. He bumped into Bakerman as the detective came to a sudden halt.

"What are we looking for, anyway?"

"My girl," Jerry said.

"She ain't your girl, kid," Bakerman said, heavy with doubt. "You ain't really married to her."

"I will be," Jerry said. "I hope to be."

Bakerman eyed him curiously, then moved forward again, into the living room. He suddenly stumbled and went

356

down on his knees with a muffled curse. There came further scraping sounds as Bakerman regained his feet, breathing heavily. His flashlight splashed suddenly across the shadowed room.

"It's that Dr. Polders."

He lay on his face, his arms and legs curiously sprawled. A little pool of blood had collected under him. There was no sign of the dagger spoke from the sunburst mirror.

Jerry asked softly: "Is he dead?"

"Naw. He's still breathing." The big cop sprayed his light over the disheveled room, on the desk with its telephone, and the overturned chair nearby. The concertina was no longer on the desk. The big detective added casually: "Your girl's here, too, Jerry."

Jerry said hoarsely: "If she's been hurt — "

"She'll be all right. Just a rap on the noggin," said Bakerman. He took a deep breath. "But I don't blame you for feeling the way you do about her.

She's an all-right dame."

Jerry dropped down beside Stephanie's still figure, lifted her head. There was a swelling bruise on her forehead, but no further evidence of injury. Her dark hair was a cloud of soft perfume as he held her in his arms. She was breathing lightly and evenly, and even as he held her, he felt her stir and her eyelids fluttered.

He put her down and stood up abruptly, not wanting to wait until she came to.

"I'll go downstairs and get some help," he said.

Bakerman said: "Don't you want to stay with her?"

"I'll be right back."

There was a little matter of catching a murderer, he decided, before he began asking Stephanie too many questions.

24

MRS. QUARLES was a long time answering Jerry's ring. He pressed the button twice, listening to the vague sounds of conversation from the lobby below. He tried to shrug off a feeling of vast depression as Mrs. Quarles' stolid footsteps approached the door.

She was fully dressed this time in a tweed suit of drab brown, and she looked at him with liquid dark eyes that had no meaning in them at all. Her big figure blocked the way inside.

She said flatly: "I've been wondering what happened to you. The police must have been quite a nuisance."

"They're going to be a big help now," Jerry said. "I want to talk to you, and I think I'd better tell you that I've found Stephanie Farley. And she's alive."

The corners of her mouth tightened a little. Her eyes were the color of ripe plums. Her long white hands made a fluttering gesture.

"I'll have to talk to you inside again," Jerry said.

"Why talk to me, young man?"

"You know why," Jerry said. "You know all the whys and hows of it."

Mrs. Quarles stared at him for a moment, then said quietly: "Very well," and stood aside to let him in. The rococo living room wasn't quite as crowded as the last time. The fringed purple lamps were still there, with the mountains of silk cushions, but most of the pictures were gone from the walls, leaving pale rectangles on the flowered paper. Most of the bric-a-brac had also disappeared. There was a wood fire burning in the fireplace, and the air was acrid with the smell of burnt paper. Jerry paused, looked at the big woman, and said:

"I'm going to search this place."

"Have you a warrant?" she asked quietly.

He said: "Would you rather I call the police up here and let them do it for me?"

"But I don't know what you expect to find."

Jerry considered the creases in his battered hat. He said thoughtfully: "I expect to find Queen Madge. A detective friend of mine told me quite a bit about a woman who was once known as Queen Madge." He looked at Mrs. Quarles. "May I search now?"

She stepped aside. He snapped on the lights as he went, aware of a chill feeling on the back of his neck. In the bedroom he found two battered pigskin valises, half packed and open. On top of one, nestled among white cotton slips, was the framed picture of Mrs. Quarles in her youth, when a morphine addict. Jerry tucked it under his arm and continued his search. The medicine chest in the bathroom was thoroughly cleaned out. There were no towels on any of the racks. An empty trunk stood on its end in the middle of the kitchen floor.

Five minutes later, he went back into the bathroom. The bathtub was set two inches away from the tiled wall, with a flat wooden ledge between to cover the gap. Jerry got down on his hands and knees and peered under the old-fashioned tub.

When he stood up, he held the missing spike from the sunburst mirror — the weapon that had killed two men. There was still some evidence of blood on it.

He went back into the living room. Mrs. Quarles was sitting close to the fire. She had pulled aside the copper screen allowing access to the flames. A red concertina lay on the floor beside her, considerably larger than the one Jerry had purchased in the pawn shop. The bellows were slashed open, and from where he stood he could see it was stuffed with currency. As he paused, he saw the woman take a thousand-dollar bill and drop it into the flames. The green currency flared up and vanished in a puff of smoke.

He felt as if he were walking in a nightmare.

Mrs. Quarles spoke to him without turning around.

"Sit down, young man. I'll be through in a minute."

"Are you going to burn all of it?" he asked quietly.

"If you will let me."

"It's evidence," he said. He slid the framed picture of Mrs. Quarles on the floor beside her, and pulled the concertina away. The big woman didn't try to stop him. Wads of currency were stuffed into the bellows, but it was surprising how little space it took to hold four hundred thousand dollars. Mrs. Quarles sat back in her chair with a sigh and folded her hands in her lap.

"I noticed you were packing," Jerry said. "You thought of going away?"

"I hoped to."

He took the dagger spike from his pocket and balanced it in the palm of his hand. Mrs. Quarles' dark eyes flickered, regarding the prismatic blade.

"I found this behind your bathtub," Jerry said.

"Indeed."

"It was not too secure a hiding place."

"Obviously. I did not put it there."

Jerry felt a tingling sensation on the back of his neck.

"This detective friend of mine," he began, "had no description of Queen Madge, who once headed an old narcotics syndicate. But an artist once told him that in her youth she looked like a Greek statue, done by the ancient Greek sculptor, Policlitus." Jerry had an urge to swallow. "A woman of heroic proportions. Like you must have been, when you were young."

Mrs. Quarles nodded. "There is no need to drag this out, young man."

Jerry said: "You were Queen Madge."

"That's true."

"How long did you know Frank Hamilton?"

"I had known him for several years before that picture was taken," she said. She paused in thought, and in the momentary silence the crackling of the fire sounded loud and spiteful. "I think there is something you ought to know. It's about Stephanie."

"I know what it is," Jerry said. "Stephanie told me that Frank Hamilton warned her repeatedly about divulging her identity to anyone. And when Johnny Lisbon learned something about her, through her photograph and birth certificate, he tried to blackmail Hamilton. Stephanie was a weak link in Hamilton's armor. His enemies knew they could injure him by action through her. The only logical explanation for such a threat is the fact that Stephanie is Frank Hamilton's daughter."

"Yes," Mrs. Quarles nodded. "He was her father."

The woman's tone was matter-of-fact, heavy with a long sadness that reached back into a dim and tragic past.

"And that isn't all," Jerry said. He took the sheaf of caricatures he had drawn of all the suspects in the case, and selected two. "I am a cartoonist, Mrs. Quarles. The prime element in any caricature is to reveal basic characteristics. I made one of you, and one of Stephanie. There was a remarkable similarity between you two. You are her mother."

Mrs. Quarles sat up straighter, her mouth tight.

"You didn't tell her this?"

"No. She doesn't know."

"She doesn't know anything about me, you see," the big woman whispered. "I never wanted her to know."

Jerry felt all the pieces of the puzzle fit snugly in his mind. It was still difficult to believe that this woman with the dark, tragic eyes was Stephanie's mother. He felt helpless in the face of her deep, hidden grief.

Lucy Quarles said quietly: "Frank

Hamilton wanted nothing more to do with me. That's why he never told her I was her mother. She thought her mother was dead. But you see, no matter what Stephanie might have discovered about these murders, I could never hurt her, even though she found me out about Frank's death."

Jerry took a deep breath.

"Did you kill Frank Hamilton?"

Lucy Quarles said quietly: "I suppose I did."

★ ★ ★

From outside came the sudden trampling of feet, the sound of Dulcey's sharp voice, and then the slam of a door at the end of the corridor. Jerry waited until silence flowed back into the room again, frowning at the money at his feet. Mrs. Quarles sat motionless, studying the fire. He felt shocked and confused by her clam confession.

After a moment he said:

"But you didn't kill Hamilton for the money."

"Of course not. Would I be burning it otherwise?" The big woman almost smiled. "I was not interested in the money, although all the others were."

"Then why burn it at all?" Jerry asked.

"Because it is evil," she said. "Because it was his." She touched her photograph with the toe of a high button shoe. "I wanted to kill him. First he made me into the woman known as Queen Madge, then into the girl in this picture — miserable, suffering. He finally organized a narcotics ring and used me to front for him. Then he got me to taking morphine, while I was peddling it. He dragged me into the whole horrible business and I was a hopeless addict myself before I got out. He made me do things I want to forget, but cannot."

She was silent a moment, her face drawn.

"When I was quite lost," Mrs.

Quarles added, "he deserted me and took our baby girl with him. I was sunk so low then that I didn't care. I finally cured myself, and I never forgot a minute of it. I thought of all the other poor souls he had sent through the same purgatory, and I decided he shouldn't be allowed to live. He didn't deserve to walk the earth."

Jerry cleared his throat.

"And you waited all these years to kill him?"

"At first I wanted to kill him, yes; but I couldn't find him. I had no idea what he had done with Stephanie, meanwhile. Then, quite by chance, after I lost contact with him for many years, he moved into that apartment below me. I don't think I wanted to kill him any more, after all that time, and I wouldn't have done anything if he had left Stephanie alone. He never recognized me, of course. I — I'm quite changed from the girl he used to know." Mrs. Quarles brought her head up sharply. "But then I saw Stephanie

369

visiting him and learned she was my own daughter, getting entangled in his evil schemes — "

Jerry said: "Do you mean that Stephanie was mixed up in his rackets, willingly?"

Mrs. Quarles shivered. "I didn't know. But you can imagine how I felt. I was afraid he would drag that poor child into his ugly life, just as he had done to me. It revived my loathing for him and I decided that he shouldn't have the chance to ruin her life, too. So I decided to kill him." She paused. "I tried to kill him two weeks ago, but he was very strong. And something else happened — "

"Wait a minute," Jerry frowned. "What about John Lisbon?"

Mrs. Quarles sighed. "He was a little too clever, because he tried to match wits with Frank. He lost, of course."

"Oh, yes. I would have killed Mr. Lisbon, anyway, if Frank hadn't." The big woman spoke without passion. "You see, Lisbon quarreled with Frank over Patti Duggan, and besides, Lisbon was a specter out of Frank's old days. He found Frank respectable, a realtor, a front man as 'The Investor' for the Cosa Nostra and other mobsters with too much money to account for to the government. Lisbon wanted to cut in. He saw Stephanie visiting here, learned she was Hamilton's daughter, and threatened to hurt her unless Hamilton gave up the Duggan girl and split some of the funds he was siphoning off from the investments for his own use. Frank never let anyone get an advantage over him. He killed Lisbon and tried to pass off Lisbon's body as his own, so he could disappear. He might have succeeded, too, if I hadn't intervened."

"How do you know all this?"

The big woman pointed to a hot-air grill in the wall. "This is an old house. Through that grill, I can hear almost every word that's said downstairs. I heard all of Frank's deals with Finchley and de Ordas and Chalett, and I heard the quarrel with Lisbon that ended in Lisbon's death. That's how I knew you had discovered Gantredi's body, too."

Jerry frowned. "Then Hamilton murdered Johnny Lisbon first, before you entered the picture?"

"It should be quite clear by now, young man," said Lucy Quarles. "I wanted to rid the world of his evil, and I tried to kill him the day after the Lisbon murder. Hamilton had already arranged for the mutilation of Lisbon's body and his own disappearance after the police accepted Lisbon's corpse as his own. I confronted Hamilton with my true identity but I won't go into the scene that followed. You can imagine his reaction. I had a gun, and in the heat of the quarrel he tried to get it away from me. You see, in his anger, he threatened to take Stephanie with him into hiding. I would not have attacked him otherwise. We struggled for the gun, and I managed to hit him over the head with it. I was ready to kill him, then, but he wasn't completely unconscious. He told me I was mistaken, that he had taken care of Stephanie all her life, sent her to excellent boarding schools, to college, and never intended to drag her into his own criminal world. He told me he had only threatened to do that because I had reappeared again. He thought I would interfere with his plans to keep Stephanie in ignorance of her background. I suppose it was the only fine thing he ever tried to do in his life, and something happened to my own anger when he told me about it. I couldn't just leave him there to die, then. So I got him into Dr. Polders' hospital."

Lucy Quarles stared unwinkingly at the fireplace.

"I nursed him at the hospital; I felt a little sorry for him, seeing him weak and helpless after all those years of ruthless strength. When he disappeared that morning, though, I knew he would come here for the money. I didn't know anything about Gantredi's offering the apartment for rent. But I heard you and Stephanie find Gantredi's body, and I knew at the same time that Frank was up on the third floor; I'd been up there and put him to bed, although he was unconscious again when I found him."

"Just a moment," Jerry said. "I'd like to know about Stephanie, and what happened to her tonight."

"Stephanie suspected that these things had happened because of her. She had hidden the concertina upstairs, and tonight she returned and telephoned me, told me she had it and the money. My name, Lucy, is painted on that concertina and she connected it with me. Frank had painted it on there many, many years ago, although I can't understand why he had kept it all this time. I — I didn't know what to do. I couldn't tell her I was her mother. It would shock her and make her bitterly unhappy. I went up there with no plan in mind, and found Polders threatening her. He was about to kill her — for the money, of course — and I stopped him, and he accidentally shot himself. Then I put Stephanie out of the way. I needed time to think. She isn't badly hurt, you'll see. I just wanted a chance to get away from here — and then she'd never know I was her mother."

"She still doesn't suspect that?" Jerry asked.

"No, but she knows I was connected with Frank somehow," said Lucy Quarles quietly. "I think it best that she should never know. You must promise me that."

Jerry said: "I think she should know the truth."

Mrs. Quarles said: "Perhaps I've been wrong, but that's why I've done what I have done." She sighed and looked at the fire. The flames cracked softly, lighting her tired face. She looked contented. "I guess that is all, young man."

"Not quite," Jerry said.

She looked at him, her dark eyes curious.

"There are still a few questions," he went on. "For instance, did you know where Frank kept his business records?"

"I think they were on microfilm in the mirror frame."

Jerry nodded. "And you knew about the spike?"

"I replaced it myself when I hid Gantredi's body."

"But who used the spike on Gantredi, in the first place?"

"I don't know," Lucy Quarles said.

"Wasn't it you?"

She seemed annoyed. "No, of course not."

"You didn't kill Gantredi?"

"No."

Jerry stood up. He said flatly: "Then you didn't kill Hamilton, either."

Mrs. Quarles folded her hands in her lap.

"But I am responsible for his death," she said. "No man could have killed Frank Hamilton with a dagger, if he had been well and strong. He was a terrifically powerful man, and it was my original attack on him that made him an easy victim for the one who actually stabbed him. Morally, I am guilty."

Jerry swallowed complete utter astonishment and began to grin. He felt unutterably relieved.

"Then you didn't actually stab Hamilton that night?"

"Why, no. Not at all."

"Do you know who did?"

She stared at him. "I thought you knew."

"I do, but — "

There came a sudden thunderous knocking on the door. Dulcey's voice pierced into the room from outside.

"Benedict! Open up in there!"

Jerry glanced at Lucy Quarles. The big woman nodded, and he went to the door and opened it, backing away from the tide of people that surged into the cluttered Victorian apartment. Dulcey charged in first, gun in hand, followed by Bakerman, Pease and

Lucius McConaughy. Stephanie was being helped by the fat editor of the *Globe*. She looked pale and worried. Wanda Dykes and Chalett followed, then Finchley and Apple, herded by a blue-coated policeman. Out in the corridor, two white-clad attendants were taking Dr. Polders down the corridor on a hospital stretcher. His eyes were open, staring glumly and dully at the ceiling.

Dulcey's hand was hard on Jerry's arm.

He said grimly: "So you kept the murderer up here while the rest of us chased around in a three-ring circus."

"Do you mean Lucy Quarles?" Jerry asked.

Dulcey stared at the money on the floor in front of the fireplace. The spike Jerry had found in the bathroom lay glittering among the packets of currency.

"You found all this here, didn't you?" Dulcey demanded.

"Sure," Jerry said. "But Lucy Quarles

didn't kill anybody."

He looked around the crowded room, and added:

"But the murderer is in this apartment with us now."

25

DULCEY said skeptically: "All right, go ahead."

For a moment, the only sound in the room was the soft crackling of the fire. Apple was tensely upright on the cushions next to Finchley. Chalett sat in a wing chair, with Bakerman and Pease flanking him. Lucy Quarles remained on the couch, Stephanie seated beside her. Their eyes watched Jerry curiously as he put his own concertina carefully to one side.

"We won't need this," he said. He looked tall and angular, his red hair touched by the fire glow behind him. "I guess, though, we'd better start at the beginning, with all this money."

McConaughy said hoarsely: "Don't forget the one-star edition, Jerry. We hit the street in two hours."

Jerry nodded. "You all know about

Hamilton's plan to take racket currency from Finchley, and from Chalett's gambling profits, and exchange the big bills for de Ordas' small currency. Four hundred thousand dollars isn't to be sneezed at. Especially by Chalett, whose prestige was at stake, or by Finchley, who is pressed to the wall financially and *had* to have the deal go through, or be ruined."

Finchley adjusted his spectacles. He still looked like an elf. Chalett maintained a scornful silence.

"Or maybe," Jerry said. "I'd better start with John Lisbon. Lisbon worked for Hamilton, but there was friction between them over Patti Duggan, and because Johnny wanted a larger cut of Hamilton's rackets. So Lisbon tried to shake down Hamilton. First of all, he'd worked for Hamilton for twenty years, and he knew about enough crimes in the past to ruin Frank. Then he learned that Steve was Hamilton's daughter and that Hamilton was deeply concerned about her. He investigated by taking

381

Steve out on dates now and then, and finally he stole one of her pictures and checked on her birth-place."

Stephanie's dark blue eyes flickered. "I never knew what he was up to until it was too late."

"Johnny Lisbon was a smart apple," Jerry nodded. "In order to get Patti back and cut into Hamilton's pie, he threatened to broadcast Steve's identity. Hamilton decided Lisbon was too big a nuisance and had to be shut up. In the heat of the quarrel, Hamilton took the easiest way and killed him. Mrs. Quarles was an indirect witness to the crime."

Dulcey snorted. "And why did Frank mutilate Lisbon's body?"

"For two reasons," Jerry pointed out. "First he was already under investigation by the Securities and Exchange Commission, facing indictment, and the federal tax people were also getting curious about his real estate manipulations to pour racket money into legitimate businesses and enterprises. If he could convince the police that he was dead, the whole case would be dropped. Then, if he could disappear, he had a chance to swipe all the money he'd collected from Finchley, Chalett, and de Ordas. When Patti Duggan identified the body as Lisbon's, I was sure that Hamilton was still alive, somewhere."

McConaughy moved ponderously across the room and seated himself with one hand on the telephone.

"Lucy Quarles disrupted Hamilton's scheme," Jerry added. "She knew of the Lisbon murder and Hamilton's plan to disappear, and, more important than the fact that she was Hamilton's wife, betrayed long ago when she was Queen Madge, she was — and is — Stephanie's mother."

Lucy Quarles accepted the disclosure without bitterness. Wanda Dykes said something obscene. Stephanie's reaction pleased Jerry. She was shocked and completely surprised, but she did not lose her poise. She stared, white-faced, from Jerry to Mrs. Quarles.

Mrs. Quarles said dimly: "I didn't want you to know. I'm sorry he thought it necessary to tell you like this."

"Why, I don't mind," Stephanie whispered. She touched her own face with slim, wondering hands. "I'm glad of it. I — "

Dulcey said harshly: "So what of it, Benedict? What's that got to do with it?"

"Just this," Jerry said, grateful for the interruption. "Lucy was afraid that Hamilton would drag Steve into crime just as he had done with her, and that reawakened her old dream for revenge. Just look at the situation — she could kill Frank *safely*, that is — and prepared for his own disappearance."

"Then she *did* kill Hamilton," Dulcey puzzled.

"She tried to," Jerry nodded. "And then she took him secretly to Polders' hospital. As far as the police were concerned then, Hamilton was dead and gone."

Dulcey said: "We had our own ideas about that."

"You suspected Hamilton was still alive, sure. But actually, only a few people knew the real truth. There was Dr. Polders, of course, and Mrs. Quarles. Then Wanda found out, when Hamilton recovered and mentioned her name and had Polders call her. And through Wanda, Apple and Chalett learned the secret. Stephanie knew he was still alive too, because Chalett made her identify Lisbon's body as Hamilton. But she didn't know anything about the hospital. Only de Ordas and Finchley were convinced that Hamilton was dead."

The little elf licked his lips and nodded, adjusted his glasses. "If I had only known . . ."

"But you didn't," Jerry said. "So you kept on looking for the money. So did the others, letting Hamilton live because if they couldn't find the money through their own efforts, they hoped to learn where it was from Hamilton."

Dulcey snapped: "Let's get to the point. I want to know who killed Gantredi."

Jerry nodded. "Gantredi was killed with a spike from the sunburst mirror frame. Didn't it strike you odd that just one of the rays *happened* to be loose, to provide a weapon for what was obviously an impromptu murder? It seemed to me there should be a reason for that spoke being loose, and I found the reason. I found a piece of microfilm on the floor under the mirror, almost as soon as I first got into that apartment. The murderer saw me pick it up, too. But it wasn't until after I found Gantredi that I investigated the socket in the frame. It was deep enough to hold several rolls of microfilm. It was an ideal safe for Hamilton to keep what business records he had.

"The murderer, in making one last search that day, found that loose spike and the microfilm. He thought it would provide a clue to the missing money. But while he stood there, spike in hand, Gantredi came in and surprised him. It was an impulsive murder, and Gantredi was only an innocent bystander, who stumbled on the killer when the murderer thought he had, at last, found the key that would get him the money. Then Mrs. Quarles learned that Gantredi was dead. When I went out to call McConaughy the first time, she came down and hid the body in the cellar. She didn't want Stephanie involved, and later she tried to persuade me to take her out of the house. At the same time, she replaced the spike in the mirror frame."

Wanda Dykes crossed her shapely legs.

"Where was Hamilton all this time?"

"Upstairs, on the third floor. Actually, I don't think he was in such bad shape as he pretended to be. I think he heard Apple and Polders who worked for Frank in the old drug ring days, conspiring to lease the apartment and search for the money, and he lit out. I knew someone was up there on the extension phone, because I heard the click when he listened in. That's why I went out for a public phone to call McConaughy.

"The murderer stole the spike a second time when the lights went out. Remember, he saw me pick up that scrap of film. Having been surprised the first time by Gantredi, he must have wondered if there was any more film still in the mirror frame. So he blew the fuses and pulled out the spike again and searched some more. He only had a moment, though, until Steve and I came out of the kitchen. He couldn't have gotten far before I hit the lobby.

"Maybe the murderer ran upstairs. He still had the spike in his hand — maybe he planned to plant it somewhere, to frame someone. Matter of fact, that's what he did a little later on — plant it in Lucy's bathroom."

"How do you know that?" Dulcey growled.

Jerry eyed the crowded room. "The

medical examiner said Hamilton died approximately at the time when the fuses blew out. When I got upstairs, Hamilton had only been dead a minute or two. But I had spent several minutes to circle the block. So Hamilton was killed while I was on my way around. Meanwhile, in the house at the time, was Finchley, in the lobby, and Mrs. Quarles, Steve — and de Ordas, outside on the street."

Finchley said: "I don't like this. I'm not so sure I intend to stay and listen to all this theorizing."

"You'll stay," Jerry said flatly. "Let's take each one of these people and see what they were doing. Mrs. Quarles went down into the cellar to replace the fuse. Steve had gone outside, to the corner, to follow me. De Ordas saw her come out — and incidentally, saw no one else go in, which limits the possibilities to the people I've named. De Ordas himself was outside, or he wouldn't have known about Steve's movements. And the murderer couldn't have escaped through the Waverly Walk entrance when I came down from the third floor, or de Ordas, Steve and Lucy Quarles would have seen him on his way out."

Finchley stood up, trembling.

"But I didn't see anyone, either."

"I know you didn't," Jerry said.

"But that means — "

"Exactly," Jerry said. "You killed Frank Hamilton."

The little man made a sound in his throat, pulled off his glasses, and turned indignantly toward Dulcey.

"Must I stay here and listen to all this?" he demanded.

"It listens good to me," Dulcey grunted.

"But I didn't even know he was alive!" His voice was a high, womanish scream. "Benedict said so himself!"

"So I did," Jerry agreed. "But while I circled the block, you went straight up to the third floor, to search further for the money. Of everybody involved, you knew of the spike — you're the one who saw me pick up that scrap of film — and you're the only one who had the opportunity to go directly upstairs. The fact that you didn't know Hamilton was alive proves my case. Normally you would never have dared tackle Hamilton, who was a powerful man. But he was weak, half conscious, when you stumbled on him up on the third floor. You already believed you had the key to the money, in the microfilm, but you weren't too sure. And when you suddenly came face to face with Hamilton, you got the shock of your life. With the spike in your hand, you behaved exactly as a man of your temperament would — you struck out in shock and rage against the one obstacle to finding that money — which was Hamilton, alive. You planted Wanda Dykes' scarf to incriminate her, you slugged me when I found the body, and you put the spike in Mrs. Quarles' bathroom. Then you went downstairs and joined de

Ordas and Stephanie in the first floor apartment."

There was silence in the room. Finchley's eyes flickered back and forth.

"You can't prove it," he whispered. "It's all theory."

"Is it?" Jerry asked. "I'm betting right now that you still have that microfilm in your coat pocket!"

Instinctively, Finchley's left hand slapped his side. Bakerman growled and reached for the little man. Finchley gasped and twisted away, snapping something toward the fire — and Jerry bent over and caught it as it went between his legs.

Finchley sobbed. "I didn't mean to — I was surprised — "

Jerry stepped away from the fireplace and handed a small roll of film to Dulcey.

"This will tell you all about Hamilton's past dealings." He quickly intercepted Finchley before he reached the door, and took the sobbing little man toward the police lieutenant. "You can take this away, too."

It was nearly dawn before Jerry found himself alone with Stephanie. The first-floor apartment was littered with cigarette butts, ashes, and scribbled papers. Somewhere a clock chimed softly, five times. McConaughy was the last to go, after the police had departed, taking Lucy Quarles with them for a signed statement. The fat editor stayed on, helping Jerry as he rapped out a carefully edited story over the telephone to the *Globe's* rewrite desk. When it was all tied up and put to bed, McConaughy paused ponderously in the doorway.

"Tullen's back from his vacation," he said. "That means you go back to cartoons tomorrow, Jerry. Not that you didn't do a hell of a fine job — although when Bakerman mentioned Queen Madge, it was natural to think of Mrs. Quarles."

"Natural, hell," said Jerry. "I notice you didn't think about her. We still wouldn't know about Stephanie's identity, if it weren't for my doodling cartoons."

McConaughy waved his cigar placidly. "We got the Lisbons all sewed up — that family was out strictly for revenge, and as long as you don't press charges I guess nothing happens to them. The same goes for Chalett, too; he's out almost two hundred grand in unreported income, and it's not likely he'll claim it with the Treasury Department waiting to ask a lot of income-tax questions. Polders will pay for his attack on Stephanie, but he's just a high-flying opportunist trying to snatch what he thought was some easy dollars. He'll survive that slug in the side."

"There's just one thing," McConaughy went on. "Dulcey is pretty sore at you. He won't try to pin anything on Lucy Quarles or the *Globe* will make his face red as hell. I'll have her back here by morning. Dulcey can't touch you or Bakerman either, for going over his head. *But* — " McConaughy waggled a fat, pink finger at Jerry and the girl — "if he ever finds out that you two are staying here without benefit of clergy — !"

Stephanie looked perfectly composed. She was lovely, Jerry thought; he had never seen anyone lovelier. He still got butterflies when he looked at her.

"I'll move out," he said. "I wouldn't want to do anything illegitimate."

McConaughy lifted mild eyebrows. "One more thing that might interest you. They picked up Pedro de Ordas an hour ago, while you were busy with the story. Found him in a downtown hotel, with an empty bottle of sleeping pills beside him. Dead as a mackerel, he was. That's a funny thing, isn't it? I should think — "

The fat man interrupted himself. The girl and Jerry were paying no attention to him. Sighing, McConaughy quietly left the apartment to them.

Jerry didn't move as Stephanie sat down beside him on the couch. He was astounded when she quietly turned to him and kissed him. His arms went around her and then he felt her body grow taut.

"You've got lipstick on your ear," she said coldly.

"Oh, that?" he thought frantically, then recalled that Wanda Dykes had tried to kiss him earlier in the evening, before he went into the house. Apparently she had scored a near miss on his ear. "That's possible," he said.

"Possible, indeed!"

He grinned. "You're making noises like a wife, Steve."

She looked thoughtfully around the quiet apartment, and then came back into his arms as if she belonged there.

"Come to think of it," she said, "that's a possibility, too."

Other titles in the Linford Mystery Library:

A GENTEEL LITTLE MURDER
Philip Daniels

Gilbert had a long-cherished plan to murder his wife. When the polished Edward entered the scene Gilbert's attitude was suddenly changed.

DEATH AT THE WEDDING
Madelaine Duke

Dr. Norah North's search for a killer takes her from a wedding to a private hospital.

MURDER FIRST CLASS
Ron Ellis

Will Detective Chief Inspector Glass find the Post Office robbers before the Executioner gets to them?

A FOOT IN THE GRAVE
Bruce Marshall

About to be imprisoned and tortured in Buenos Aires, John Smith escapes, only to become involved in an aeroplane hijacking.

DEAD TROUBLE
Martin Carroll

Trespassing brought Jennifer Denning more than she bargained for. She was totally unprepared for the violence which was to lie in her path.

HOURS TO KILL
Ursula Curtiss

Margaret went to New Mexico to look after her sick sister's rented house and felt a sharp edge of fear when the absent landlady arrived.

THE DEATH OF ABBE DIDIER
Richard Grayson

Inspector Gautier of the Sûreté investigates three crimes which are strangely connected.

NIGHTMARE TIME
Hugh Pentecost

Have the missing major and his wife met with foul play somewhere in the Beaumont Hotel, or is their disappearance a carefully planned step in an act of treason?

BLOOD WILL OUT
Margaret Carr

Why was the manor house so oddly familiar to Elinor Howard? Who would have guessed that a Sunday School outing could lead to murder?

THE DRACULA MURDERS
Philip Daniels

The Horror Ball was interrupted by a spectral figure who warned the merrymakers they were tampering with the unknown.

THE LADIES
OF LAMBTON GREEN
Liza Shepherd

Why did murdered Robin Colquhoun's picture pose such a threat to the ladies of Lambton Green?

CARNABY
AND THE GAOLBREAKERS
Peter N. Walker

Detective Sergeant James Aloysius Carnaby-King is sent to prison as bait. When he joins in an escape he is thrown headfirst into a vicious murder hunt.

MUD IN HIS EYE
Gerald Hammond

The harbourmaster's body is found mangled beneath Major Smyle's yacht. What is the sinister significance of the illicit oysters?

THE SCAVENGERS
Bill Knox

Among the masses of struggling fish in the *Tecta*'s nets was a larger, darker, ominously motionless form . . . the body of a skin diver.

DEATH IN ARCADY
Stella Phillips

Detective Inspector Matthew Furnival works unofficially with the local police when a brutal murder takes place in a caravan camp.

STORM CENTRE
Douglas Clark

Detective Chief Superintendent Masters, temporarily lecturing in a police staff college, finds there's more to the job than a few weeks relaxation in a rural setting.

THE MANUSCRIPT MURDERS
Roy Harley Lewis

Antiquarian bookseller Matthew Coll, acquires a rare 16th century manuscript. But when the Dutch professor who had discovered the journal is murdered, Coll begins to doubt its authenticity.

SHARENDEL
Margaret Carr

Ruth didn't want all that money. And she didn't want Aunt Cass to die. But at Sharendel things looked different. She began to wonder if she had a split personality.

MURDER TO BURN
Laurie Mantell

Sergeants Steven Arrow and Lance Brendon, of the New Zealand police force, come upon a woman's body in the water. When the dead woman is identified they begin to realise that they are investigating a complex fraud.

YOU CAN HELP ME
Maisie Birmingham

Whilst running the Citizens' Advice Bureau, Kate Weatherley is attacked with no apparent motive. Then the body of one of her clients is found in her room.

DAGGERS DRAWN
Margaret Carr

Stacey Manston was the kind of girl who could take most things in her stride, but three murders were something different . . .

THE MONTMARTRE MURDERS
Richard Grayson

Inspector Gautier of Sûreté investigates the disappearance of artist Théo, the heir to a fortune.

GRIZZLY TRAIL
Gwen Moffat

Miss Pink, alone in the Rockies, helps in a search for missing hikers, solves two cruel murders and has the most terrifying experience of her life when she meets a grizzly bear!

BLINDMAN'S BLUFF
Margaret Carr

Kate Deverill had considered suicide. It was one way out — and preferable to being murdered.

BEGOTTEN MURDER
Martin Carroll

When Susan Phillips joined her aunt on a voyage of 12,000 miles from her home in Melbourne, she little knew their arrival would germinate the seeds of murder planted long ago.

WHO'S THE TARGET?
Margaret Carr

Three people whom Abby could identify as her parents' murderers wanted her dead, but she decided that maybe Jason could have been the target.

THE LOOSE SCREW
Gerald Hammond

After a motor smash, Beau Pepys and his cousin Jacqueline, her fiancé and dotty mother, suspect that someone had prearranged the death of their friend. But who, and why?

CASE WITH THREE HUSBANDS
Margaret Erskine

Was it a ghost of one of Rose Bonner's late husbands that gave her old Aunt Agatha such a terrible shock and then murdered her in her bed?

THE END OF THE RUNNING
Alan Evans

Lang continued to push the men and children on and on. Behind them were the men who were hunting them down, waiting for the first signs of exhaustion before they pounced.

CARNABY AND THE HIJACKERS
Peter N. Walker

When Commander Pigeon assigns Detective Sergeant Carnaby-King to prevent a raid on a bullion-carrying passenger train, he knows that there are traitors in high positions.

TREAD WARILY AT MIDNIGHT
Margaret Carr

If Joanna Morse hadn't been so hasty she wouldn't have been involved in the accident.

TOO BEAUTIFUL TO DIE
Martin Carroll

There was a grave in the churchyard to prove Elizabeth Weston was dead. Alive, she presented a problem. Dead, she could be forgotten. Then, in the eighth year of her death she came back. She was beautiful, but she had to die.

IN COLD PURSUIT
Ursula Curtiss

In Mexico, Mary and her cousin Jenny each encounter strange men, but neither of them realises that one of these men is obsessed with revenge and murder. But which one?

LITTLE DROPS OF BLOOD
Bill Knox

It might have been just another unfortunate road accident but a few little drops of blood pointed to murder.

GOSSIP TO THE GRAVE
Jonathan Burke

Jenny Clark invented Simon Sherborne because her daily gossip column was getting dull. Then Simon appeared at a party — in the flesh! And Jenny finds herself involved in murder.

HARRIET FAREWELL
Margaret Erskine

Wealthy Theodore Buckler had planned a magnificent Guy Fawkes Day celebration. He hadn't planned on murder.